Nikki stepped for[ward], [her]
bare toes nudged [against his]
palm of her hand [...........] [his]
balance and rose on tiptoe to kiss the
underside of his chin.

Cully's eyes narrowed, his heart thudding faster beneath her palm. "Don't do that unless you mean it."

"I mean it," she whispered.

"Does this mean you're done thinking about us?"

"Yes."

"And what have you decided?"

"That I've wasted a lot of time thinking."

Cully smiled slowly, his eyes going dark. "It's about damn time." He set his coffee mug on the porch railing and bent to slip an arm under her legs, swinging her off her feet and into his arms.

Nikki gasped and clutched at him, gaining a fistful of shirt. "Where are you taking me?"

"Where you belong," he said, his voice raspy, deeper. "To bed."

Dear Reader,

Spring is a time for new beginnings. And as you step out to enjoy the spring sunshine, I'd like to introduce a new author to Silhouette Special Edition. Her name is Judy Duarte, and her novel *Cowboy Courage* tells the heartwarming story of a runaway heiress who finds shelter in the strong arms of a handsome—yet guarded—cowboy. Don't miss this brilliant debut!

Next, we have the new installment in Susan Mallery's DESERT ROGUES miniseries. In *The Sheik & the Virgin Princess,* a beautiful princess goes in search of her long-lost royal father, and on her quest falls in love with her heart-meltingly gorgeous bodyguard! And love proves to be the irresistible icing in this adorable tale by Patricia Coughlin, *The Cupcake Queen.* Here, a lovable heroine turns her hero's life into a virtual beehive. But Cupid's arrow does get the final—er—sting!

I'm delighted to bring you Crystal Green's *His Arch Enemy's Daughter*, the next story in her poignant miniseries KANE'S CROSSING. When a rugged sheriff falls for the wrong woman, he has to choose between revenge and love. Add to the month Pat Warren's exciting new two-in-one, *My Very Own Millionaire*— two fabulous romances in one novel about confirmed bachelors who finally find the women of their dreams! Lastly, there is no shortage of gripping emotion (or tears!) in Lois Faye Dyer's *Cattleman's Bride-To-Be,* where long-lost lovers must reunite to save the life of a little girl. As they fight the medical odds, this hero and heroine find that passion—and soul-searing love—never die....

I'm so happy to present these first fruits of spring. I hope you enjoy this month's lineup and come back for next month's moving stories about life, love and family!

Best,

Karen Taylor Richman
Senior Editor

Please address questions and book requests to:
Silhouette Reader Service
U.S.: 3010 Walden Ave., P.O. Box 1325, Buffalo, NY 14269
Canadian: P.O. Box 609, Fort Erie, Ont. L2A 5X3

Cattleman's Bride-To-Be

LOIS FAYE DYER

SPECIAL EDITION™

Published by Silhouette Books

America's Publisher of Contemporary Romance

For Lilia Rae, the most wonderful granddaughter
any grandmother could wish to have

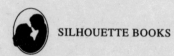 SILHOUETTE BOOKS

ISBN 0-373-24457-6

CATTLEMAN'S BRIDE-TO-BE

Copyright © 2002 by Lois Faye Dyer

This edition published by arrangement with Harlequin Books S.A.

® and TM are trademarks of Harlequin Books S.A., used under license. Trademarks indicated with ® are registered in the United States Patent and Trademark Office, the Canadian Trade Marks Office and in other countries.

Visit Silhouette at www.eHarlequin.com

Printed in U.S.A.

Books by Lois Faye Dyer

Silhouette Special Edition

Lonesome Cowboy #1038
He's Got His Daddy's Eyes #1129
The Cowboy Takes a Wife #1198
The Only Cowboy for Caitlin #1253
Cattleman's Courtship #1306
Cattleman's Bride-To-Be #1457

LOIS FAYE DYER

is the author of thirteen romance novels. She lives on Washington State's beautiful Puget Sound with her husband and their yellow Lab, Maggie Mae. She loves to hear from readers and can be reached at c/o Paperbacks Plus, 1618 Bay Street, Port Orchard, WA 98366.

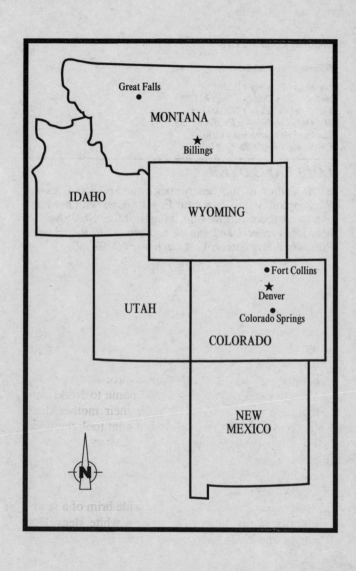

Prologue

The small ranching community of Colson, Montana, dozed under the hot summer sun. Nikki Petersen strolled down the sidewalk, a bag of groceries on one hip, her steps light as she approached her great-aunt Cora's house. The three-story, yellow Victorian mansion had become home to Nikki and her little sister, Angelica, after their mother died four years earlier and their great-aunt took them in. The big old house was shabbily genteel, the white paint fading on its gingerbread trim, but the flower gardens surrounding it glowed with brilliant color under the hot sun.

Cora, her face shaded by the wide brim of a straw hat, her sturdy form encased in a white sleeveless blouse and khaki shorts, bent over a rose bush, clippers in hand. Beside her, four-year-old Angelica held a wicker basket nearly filled with summer blooms.

"Hi!" Angelica spotted Nikki and deserted Cora to race across the lawn, glossy black braids flying, her bare legs tan beneath the hem of denim shorts.

"Hi." Nikki laughed as the little girl skidded to a stop beside her. "Careful, kiddo."

"We're cutting flowers for the parlor," Angelica informed her importantly.

"Really?" Nikki managed to look suitably impressed.

"Uh-huh. Come see." Angelica took her hand and tugged.

Nikki allowed the little girl to pull her up the walk and across the lawn. Cora braced a hand against the small of her back and winced.

"Are you all right?" Nikki frowned with concern.

"I'm fine. Just these old bones complaining. They do that when I spend too long pulling weeds and bending over to pick flowers."

Angelica tugged on Nikki's hand. "I don't have old bones," she said gravely. "Just Aunt Cora."

Nikki stifled a grin and nodded solemnly. "I see." She glanced at Cora and found her aunt's eyes alight with amusement.

"Just wait, angel-mine," Cora said. "When you're my age, your bones will ache, too." She nodded at the bag perched on Nikki's hip. "You must have found something more at the grocery store than the milk and eggs I asked for."

Nikki laughed. "Just a few things—you know me, I can't resist fresh fruit. And I remembered that I need rice and mushrooms for a new casserole recipe I want to try."

"Mmm. Sounds good. Will that be dinner tonight?"

"No, tomorrow night. I have a date tonight."

"Well." Cora smiled. "That's good news. You work much too hard—it's about time you had some fun. Who's the lucky young man?"

"Cully Bowdrie."

Cora stiffened, her smile disappearing. "I see."

The response surprised Nikki. She hadn't expected Cora to be prejudiced against Cully despite his bad-boy reputation, although in truth, she sensed a different emotion beneath Cora's brief words. An emotion Nikki couldn't quite define.

"Do you know Cully?" she asked.

"No. I haven't met him, although I've seen him a time or two. In a town the size of Colson, it's impossible not to run across most everyone in the county at one time or another." Cora glanced at Angelica. The little girl had her back to the two women, bending over to add a delicate pink rosebud to the basket of flowers. "I knew his father," she added, her tone grim.

"You knew Charlie? You never mentioned it before," Nikki murmured quietly, not wanting Angelica to overhear her. "I've heard the gossip about the Bowdries, so I know Charlie scandalized all of Colson when he had an affair and fathered Quinn and Cully. And I know his wife never forgave him.''

What she knew of Cully's stepmother, the self-proclaimed leader of Colson society, wasn't good. Eileen Bowdrie's bitterness and hatred toward Charlie, Quinn and Cully was the stuff of local legend. After Charlie's death, Eileen had moved from the ranch into town, but she continued to stir up trouble for her stepsons whenever the opportunity arose. Her vindictiveness knew no bounds. ''And I know the gossips had a field day when he brought the boys home and made his wife raise them. But do you think it's fair to hold Cully and Quinn responsible for what their parents did?''

''No, Nikki, I don't think it's fair. But, there's no denying that the Bowdrie brothers have been in and out of trouble since the day their rich daddy brought them home. If even half of the rumors I've heard about those two are true, they're still wilder than any other young men in the county. Although I'm not a big believer in rumors and gossip,'' Cora added with blunt honesty.

''Then what is it? I can tell you're not happy to learn that I'm going out with him.''

Cora's troubled gaze searched Nikki's face, then moved briefly from the crown of her head to her toes, before settling on Angelica.

Nikki knew with sudden certainty that her great-aunt was comparing her and Angelica. No two sisters could have been less alike. Angelica's mane of glossy hair was raven black, while her own hair was a deep auburn shot with gold highlights. Freckles lightly dusted her fair skin across her cheekbones and the bridge of her nose, while Angelica's skin boasted a tanned, golden sheen without a freckle in sight. The only aspects of their appearance that betrayed their connection as sisters were their brown eyes framed with dark lashes, and their long legs. Dancer's legs, Nikki's mother had once claimed, teasing her.

Cora's gaze left the sturdy little body kneeling beside the flower basket and returned to Nikki. "I wish you were dating a less…complicated young man," she said at last. "But you're twenty years old and I suppose that's old enough to be sensible about the men you see. Just be careful, okay? Cully Bowdrie's a heartbreaker."

"Don't worry, Aunt Cora. We're just going dancing. Cully's a lot of fun, but I know he's not the type to settle down. I'm certainly not going to fall in love with him."

Cora enfolded her slim, young great-niece in a swift hug. "Smart girl. See that you don't. Now let's get those groceries in the house," she said bracingly, pulling away to take one handle of the flower basket, while Angelica grasped the other in her two small hands.

Nikki followed them into the house, still unable to banish the feeling that there was something Cora wasn't telling her.

Not two months later, Nikki had cause to remember Cora's concern and her own blithe claim that she wouldn't fall in love with Cully. She followed her heart, dizzily happy, and never anticipated the circumstances that would drive her to leave Colson, Cully, Cora and Angelica behind.

Chapter One

Please, God. Let her be okay.

Nikki bent over her little sister's hospital bed. Angelica was sound asleep, one hand clutching the ragged teddy bear that had slept beside her since birth. Nikki brushed a lock of hair from the child's cheek and smoothed her palm down the length of silky black braid that lay against the pillow.

She bitterly regretted the four years she'd lived away from Angelica. That time seemed wasted when it might prove to be the last four years her little sister had on earth.

The wind picked up outside, the breeze finding its way through the open window to stir the drapes and cool the room with night air. Muted sounds of city streets at night drifted upward, reaching inside the room on the fifth floor of Denver's Adair Children's Hospital. Somewhere far below, a police siren grew louder before fading away, leaving only occasional traffic noise in its wake.

Nikki glanced at her watch: 3:00 a.m. Even the hardiest of Denver's citizens must be sleeping. How she wished she were one of them. She hadn't slept an entire night through in weeks.

Angelica stirred, moving fretfully beneath the light blanket.

"Shh." Nikki brushed the backs of her fingers soothingly over the little girl's pale cheek. "Go back to sleep, sweetie. I'm here."

Angelica sighed, pressing her face against Nikki's fingers and murmuring incoherently before settling once again.

Footsteps sounded in the hall outside, then the faint swish of the door moving inward joined the muted beep of monitors in the quiet room.

A smile of welcome curved Nikki's mouth and she glanced over her shoulder, expecting to see the night nurse on her rounds.

Far from it.

A tall man dressed in jeans, denim jacket and boots, his body tapering from wide shoulders to slim hips and long legs, stepped over the threshold. He halted just inside the room, the door easing shut quietly behind him. Beneath the brim of his white Stetson, his eyes narrowed as his gaze leveled on Nikki.

An unexpected surge of joy and bittersweet pain

swept through her before being swiftly burned away by a wave of anger.

She'd known Cullen Bowdrie would arrive sooner or later. She knew that she needed him here. But she hated knowing that she was forced to deal with him. She'd managed to avoid him for more than four years, and if that time lapse had been a lifetime, it still wouldn't have been long enough for Nikki.

"Cullen," she murmured, managing a stiff tilt of her head in greeting.

"Nikki."

His answering nod was just as brief, his deep voice as devoid of emotion as she hoped hers had been. He moved toward her, his loose-limbed stride evoking powerful memories that Nikki ruthlessly ignored.

He paused an arm's length away, tucked his hands into the back pockets of his faded, snug jeans and studied her assessingly. Nikki refused to look away from his hard stare, though she felt the impact of that green gaze as if he'd touched her.

"I wasn't expecting you tonight." Nikki spoke at last, her murmured words carefully neutral in the hushed quiet. "I didn't know that Quinn had found you."

"He didn't. I called home last night and he told me about *your sister.*"

Your sister. The emphasis in his voice was telling. *Don't lose your temper. You need his cooperation.* Nikki's fingers gripped the raised bed rail tighter. "Did he explain? About the blood tests?"

"He told me that your sister has some kind of rare blood disease and needs a donor—and that you asked him to have his blood tested. He also told me that you gave him some wild story about our father having had an affair with your mother. And that Angelica is the result."

Cully's tone left no doubt that he didn't believe the claim. Beneath the brim of his Stetson, the lines of his face seemed carved in stone, his gaze steely. Nikki refused to let her own gaze waver.

"And you don't believe me." It wasn't a question. Nikki was sure she already knew the answer, but the dismissive shrug of his shoulders confirmed his reaction. Angelica stirred, her slight body shifting beneath the sheet. Nikki glanced at her sister and stepped away from the bed. "I don't want to wake her," she whispered. "We can talk over here."

Without waiting for Cully to agree, she crossed the room to the open window. Her back to him, she stared out at the city glow that lit the dark night, her skin prickling with awareness when he joined her.

He leaned one shoulder against the wall, folded his arms across his chest and waited patiently for her to speak.

Bracing herself, she turned to face him, her gaze meeting his. "Is there a specific reason why you won't consider the possibility that your father might be Angelica's biological father?" she asked evenly, keeping her voice low.

"Yes, there is. You're the fourth woman in the

last three years to claim that a Bowdrie fathered a kid we didn't know about.'' He didn't add that one of those females had sworn that Quinn was her baby's father, nor did he mention that he himself had married the woman to buy her silence. The marriage and the birth that followed had been a disaster he refused to discuss. Instead, he only shrugged once again, although his hard gaze belied the offhand movement. ''Ever since our stepmother sued Quinn and me over Charlie's will and made it common knowledge that any of his descendants, legitimate or illegitimate, would inherit a share of the estate, women have been coming out of the woodwork with claims that their kids are half Bowdrie.''

Nikki stiffened, anger heating her cheeks. She struggled to keep her voice low. ''If you're suggesting that the reason I asked you and Quinn to have your blood tested is to prove that Angelica is entitled to a share of Charlie's estate, you're wrong.''

''Maybe. But you have to admit that it seems a little too coincidental that your aunt remembered your mother once had an affair with Charlie at the precise moment that your half sister needed expensive medical care.''

Nikki's fists clenched tighter, her fingernails digging half-moons into soft skin. ''I'm only interested in finding a bone marrow donor. I don't need your money and neither does Angelica.''

''Really?''

With the swiftness of a striking rattlesnake, Cully

reached out and caught her left hand in his. Nikki instinctively moved to pull away, but he held her fast.

"No ring." His hooded gaze flicked from her bare fingers to her face. "So you didn't marry money. What have you been doing since you ran away from Colson that brought you enough money to pay for high-cost hospital care, Nikki?"

She couldn't bear the warm touch of his callused palm beneath her fingertips. She tugged against his hold, and this time he let her go. Unfortunately, he remained standing only inches from her. The scent of night air, leather and man that was unique to Cully assaulted her senses with every breath she took. She steeled herself not to react to the memories that plagued her, and stood firm, refusing to step back.

"It's no concern of yours what I've been doing since I left Colson, Cully," she said evenly. Angelica's medical costs were being covered by a charitable organization for children afflicted with aplastic anemia, but she didn't intend to share that information with Cully. She refused to care if he thought the worst of her. "I don't owe you an explanation and I won't give you one." Despite her best efforts, bitterness seeped into her words.

"Why not? Are you ashamed of what you've been doing?" He shot back.

The banked anger that lay beneath his response was clear. Nikki ignored it.

"No, I'm not ashamed of my life in Seattle." Anger heated Nikki's cheeks and thrummed through her veins. "The only thing in my life that I'm ashamed of is the one-night stand I shared with you."

"It wasn't a one-night stand." His mouth tightened, flattening into a hard line.

"No?" Nikki lifted an eyebrow in disbelief. "We had sex once. That qualifies as a one-night stand."

"You were a virgin." He bit out. "And we didn't just have sex. We made love."

"You have an interesting memory of events, Cully. Let me tell you how I remember our prior association. Yes, I was a virgin. Yes, we had *sex*. You left before dawn, while I was asleep, with a note that you'd call me later. You didn't call. Then you showed up at the apartment two days later and stayed just long enough to tell me that you were marrying someone else." Nikki swallowed the flood of bitter betrayal that filled her, refusing to let him know how much his marriage had hurt her. "You used me, Cully. I was a one-night stand."

"Hell, you won't listen, will you?" A muscle flexed along the tense line of his jaw. "There's no talking with you when you're like this," he said flatly.

"There's no talking with me *about* this," she corrected, the antagonism in her glare matching his. "What happened between us four years ago is ancient history. All I want from you is your agreement to have your blood tested. That's all. Quinn understands that, even if you don't."

"Quinn's a pushover where kids are concerned.

He always has been, and ever since he married Victoria and they had one of their own, he's worse. He would have taken in every kid that claimed they were Charlie's if I hadn't stopped him." His gaze narrowed on her. "What Quinn didn't tell me was why he believed you."

"I don't know that he *did* believe me." Nikki briefly tried to conjure up an image of tough rancher Quinn Bowdrie being a soft touch for scheming women, but found the picture too incredible. "But he's willing to have his blood tested on the chance that he might be a bone marrow match for Angelica."

"And is he?"

"I don't know. We won't know the test results until tomorrow."

"So much for the paternity claim against Charlie." Cully shrugged in abrupt dismissal, his gaze hardening. "What about you? You're her sister. Why can't you give her what she needs?"

"Because I'm not a match." Nikki's gaze met his. "But you might be, Cully."

"If Quinn doesn't match, I won't, either."

"You might." Nikki drew a deep breath, meeting his hard stare unflinchingly. Despite the fact that he clearly thought she was lying about Angelica's connection to his father, she swallowed her anger and pride and forged ahead. "Without a bone marrow transplant, Angelica will die." Her voice wobbled, and the lump of emotion that clogged her throat made her pause before she tried again. "I don't want your money, Cully, I just want my sister to live. I don't know if my mother was lying or telling the truth when she claimed Charlie fathered Angelica. I don't care. All I know is that if there's the slightest chance that you and Quinn are related to Angelica, then there's a chance that your bone marrow might be able to save her life.''

She searched his features, but no emotion moved across his face. No acceptance, but neither could she read outright rejection. ''Please, Cully,'' she whispered, hating the weakness that roughened her voice with tears. Hating him for making her plead. ''Please do this.''

Cully absorbed her words without expression. Bracing himself internally, he did what he'd purposely avoided since he'd entered the room. He half turned to stare at the little girl on the bed.

She's so little. The knowledge hit him with the force of a blow. That a life-threatening disease raged within that small body seemed obscene. He didn't recall ever seeing her in their small hometown of Colson, Montana, and wondered if he'd ever passed her on the street. He'd occasionally nodded hello to white-haired Cora Petersen on Colson's Main Street, but he'd paid little attention to the child at her side.

He left the window and crossed the room, halting by the bed rail to stare at the child asleep on the high bed. He was aware of Nikki joining him, but the little girl claimed all his attention.

His gaze moved slowly over her face, searching for familiar features. Her hair was the same raven black as his own, but neither he nor Quinn shared her distinctive widow's peak. Her mouth was a Cupid's bow, soft and vulnerable, and neither it nor the delicate bridge of her small nose bore any resemblance to the nose and mouth he saw each day in his shaving mirror. The small hands that lay atop the blanket were small-boned, nothing like his larger, callused fingers and palms.

Could this small, delicate person really be his half sister? A wave of fierce protectiveness swamped him with unexpected strength. His body tensed to endure the slam of unwanted emotion.

"Cully," Nikki murmured softly. She hated to beg, but for Angelica's sake, she would have gone down on her knees.

He glanced from the child to Nikki, following her when she left the bedside for the window once again.

"You're the only sibling that remains untested."

"Possible sibling," he corrected. Although he fought the pull, something deep in his gut told him that an undeniable force connected him to the little girl who lay so still beneath the hospital bed's white sheet. "We don't know for sure if there's a connection."

"Okay," Nikki conceded. "Possible sibling. Nevertheless, if there's any chance at all, won't you let the hospital test you? A few minutes in the lab to have a technician draw your blood—that's all it would cost you, and it could mean life or death for Angelica."

"All right," he said abruptly. "I'm not agreeing

that Charlie was her father, but there's still a chance that an unrelated person might be a match, right?''

Nikki felt her heart stop before it resumed a rapid beat once again.

''Yes. Although the probability that you might match would be substantially less.'' Tears of relief trembled on her lashes before overflowing to trickle down her cheeks, and she wiped them away with unsteady fingertips, grateful that Cully's brooding gaze had returned to Angelica.

The quiet in the room was broken only by the beep of a monitor and the occasional sound of a nurse passing in the hall outside. Cully appeared to have forgotten her presence, and Nikki took advantage of the opportunity to watch him unobserved. She hated to admit, even to herself, that conflicting emotions surged through her. She wanted to feel nothing for Cully Bowdrie beyond anger and a thankfulness that he was willing to be tested for compatibility. She didn't want to acknowledge that the undeniable pull of male to female still existed between them.

He's thinner than the last time I saw him.

Beneath the shadow of black stubble, his cheekbones and jawline were more defined. His nose and forehead seemed more sharply etched. His eyes seemed an even deeper green in the lamplit room, his brows and lashes the same raven black as his hair, which curled against the collar of his jacket.

But the most startling change was the jagged scar that started beneath the left side of his jaw and zigzagged its way down his throat until it disappeared beneath the blue cotton of his shirt collar.

Nikki knew that Cully had been injured some three years before in the car crash that had taken his wife's life and that of their young son. He'd spent weeks in the hospital and been left with facial scars and permanent damage to one leg. But gossip hadn't prepared her for the complete personality change she saw. She didn't know what she had expected, exactly, but what she found shocked her to her soul. This man that she'd given her heart and body to one hot summer night, only to have him tell her two days later that he was marrying someone else, had become a stranger. She wasn't sure that she knew this Cully at all.

Cully Bowdrie's face remained handsome despite the physical scarring, but his easygoing, charming personality appeared to have disappeared completely, replaced by a hard, dangerous edginess.

He glanced up, pinning her gaze with his. For a moment, Nikki thought she glimpsed a brief flare of heated emotion, but then it was gone, and she decided that she must have imagined it.

"How long have you known that your mother claimed Charlie was her father?"

Given how far away from the hospital room her thoughts had traveled, his question was disorienting. She hesitated, collecting her thoughts before responding. "Not long. Aunt Cora told me when we learned that I wasn't a match and that I couldn't donate bone marrow." Nikki forced herself to answer calmly despite the suspicion written on

Cully's hard features. "My mother told her when Angelica was born, but Aunt Cora didn't believe her."

"Why not?"

Nikki shrugged. "According to Aunt Cora, my mother tended to exaggerate to create the life she wanted, and sometimes her stories were closer to fairy tales than fact. And my mother had never mentioned that she was seeing Charlie before Angelica was born, so Aunt Cora assumed that Mama simply picked out the richest man in the county and named him as the father of her child. When the doctor told us that the best hope of a close match for a donor for Angelica was a brother or sister, I told him that I was her only sibling. That's when Aunt Cora told me that there was a possibility that you and Quinn might be her half brothers."

"So this isn't something you yourself have known for years?"

"No. Not at all." Nikki shook her head in emphatic denial. "If I'd known, I would have told you, Cully."

She wasn't sure he believed her. He didn't comment.

Angelica stirred, murmuring in her sleep. Nikki quickly crossed the room to her side, soothing the little girl back into sounder sleep. Cully followed more slowly, halting next to her. Once again, silence stretched as he studied Angelica once again.

"How old is she?" he said at last.

"She turned eight on her last birthday."

"Damn," he muttered, shaking his head. "She's just a baby."

"Yes," Nikki agreed.

"If you can find a donor, what are her chances?"

"Complete recovery. Unlike some other blood diseases, aplastic anemia is curable, with the right donor and the right amount of luck." Nikki stroked Angelica's hair back from her forehead, the gesture vibrant with fierce protectiveness. "She will get well," she murmured, her voice determined. "I know she will."

If it were possible to guarantee healing through sheer force of will, Cully believed Nikki would do it. Unfortunately, Angelica required more practical assistance to raise her odds.

He tugged his Stetson lower over his brow and stepped back from the bed.

"I'm going to find a hotel room for what's left of the night, but I'll be back in the morning. Will you let her doctor know that I'm ready to be tested?"

"Yes. He usually makes his rounds between seven and seven-thirty. I'll tell him then."

"Good." He nodded and headed for the door.

"Cully?"

Her voice stopped him just as he pulled the door open. He glanced back over his shoulder. "Yeah?"

"Thank you." The words nearly stuck in her throat.

He shrugged. "Don't thank me yet. There's no guarantee that my blood will match hers."

"I know. But there's a chance." *And we're run-*

ning out of options. She didn't say the words aloud, but she had the uncanny feeling that Cully understood.

"Maybe, but don't get your hopes up. Good night."

"Good night."

He disappeared into the hall, pulling the door nearly closed behind him. Nikki stared after him for long moments. That last image of long legs and broad shoulders backlit by the hall light was engraved on her memory. At last she turned back to the bed.

"Angelica," she whispered to the sleeping child. "I pray he can save you."

But even if he was the miracle she'd prayed for, some deep instinct told her that Cully, with his scarred face and guarded eyes, had the power to threaten her own hard-won peace of mind. And that this darker Cully might pose a greater threat than the man who'd broken her heart four long years ago.

Cully strode down the deserted hall to the elevator, ignoring the curious looks from the two women at the nurses' station as he passed. He jabbed the elevator call button with his forefinger and waited impatiently until the doors slid open to let him step inside. Then he thumbed the button for the lobby, staring unseeingly at the numbers as the doors slid silently closed. When the doors opened once again, Cully exited, barely glancing at the empty lobby with its glowing lamps and comfortable groupings of sofas and chairs as he strode across the expanse of marble floor to the glass double doors.

Outside, the cool night air was a welcome relief after the hospital odor of antiseptic. Cully dragged in deep lungfuls on his way to the nearly empty parking lot where he'd left his truck.

He hated the smell of hospitals. The distinctive scent brought back unwelcome memories of the weeks he'd spent in a hospital bed while doctors repaired his broken body. At least they'd patched him back together again, he thought grimly. His wife and her two-month-old baby had died from injuries suffered in the fiery car crash.

Cully purposely used the mechanics of driving to occupy his mind as he negotiated unfamiliar city streets and checked into a hotel. It wasn't until he'd showered and was lying in bed, his hands folded beneath his head as he stared up at the dark ceiling, that he let himself think about Nikki.

She hates me.

Knowing that she had cause to blame him for the way they'd parted didn't ease the ache in his chest. He couldn't deny the bare-bones facts she'd thrown at him. Nor could he flesh out those stark facts and tell her what really had happened the morning after they'd made love. Despite the years that had passed, he couldn't share the entire truth behind his sudden marriage. That truth still had the potential to damage other people.

So many regrets, he thought grimly. So much wasted time.

The ceiling above his bed faded, and instead of white plaster, Cully's memory played back images from the moment he'd pushed open the hospital door and stepped into Angelica's room.

The slim woman bending over the bed had a mane of red-gold hair that tumbled down her back. Dressed in a simple black turtleneck sweater tucked into the waist of black jeans, her slender form stood out starkly against the gleaming white of bedsheets, curtains and walls.

She'd lifted her head and half turned to glance over her shoulder, the lamplight falling on her features. Her eyes had widened in shock, making him feel as if a giant hand had closed around his heart and squeezed. The glow of lamplight had tinted Nikki's skin a soft gold, her eyes dark beneath the delicate arch of her brows, the lush curve of her mouth vulnerable.

And when he'd crossed the room and stood next to her, the impact of those first few seconds only grew stronger. Four years had matured her, given her a self-confidence that she hadn't possessed before, but it hadn't lessened the leap of his senses whenever she was near.

Four years had passed since Nikki Petersen left Colson. He should be over her—so why did his heart hurt as if he'd just been struck in the chest?

Cully was running on a couple hours of sleep and too many mugs of black coffee when he returned to the hospital late the next morning.

Gone was the predawn quiet. The fifth-floor pediatric wing bustled with nurses, orderlies and the occasional doctor in a white lab coat.

And when Cully pushed open the door to Angelica's room, she was awake, her small body propped against pillows at the head of the bed, her chocolate-brown eyes regarding him with solemn curiosity.

Before he could speak, Nikki stepped out of the bathroom, carrying a towel in one hand, a damp washcloth in the other. She halted abruptly when she saw him.

"Oh. Hello." She glanced at Angelica, then back at Cully. "I didn't know you were here, Cully. Have you met Angelica?"

"No. I just got here."

"Nikki?"

The soft little voice interrupted whatever response Cully may have made. Nikki crossed the room to Angelica's bedside, smoothing a strand of silky hair from her cheek.

"Hi, sleepyhead. So you're awake at last. There's someone here to meet you."

Angelica's gaze left Nikki and moved to Cully.

"Hello." She studied him for a moment before a sweet smile curved her mouth. "You look like Quinn."

"That's because he's my brother." He walked across the room until he was close enough to her bed that the rolled-back sleeve of his shirt brushed the rail. "I'm Cully."

Her lashes drooped over sleepy eyes, but Cully could easily read the bone-deep weariness and suf-

fering that lay in the chocolaty depths. He felt a
surge of empathy for the child. He, too, had lain
helpless in a hospital bed, wondering if he'd live,
enduring the pain, willing the days to pass until the
torment would end and he could escape. *God. She's
so little, and way too young for this.*

"I like Quinn," she murmured, stretching out an
arm. Her little hand patted his, the small palm and
fingers catching his and drawing him closer to cud-
dle his work-roughened hand against her smooth
cheek. "He has horses. When I get out of the hospital and go home, he's going to teach me to ride,"
she confided. "Do you have horses?"

"Yeah." Cully struggled to speak past the lump
in his throat. She hadn't questioned him. With simple childish faith, she'd reached out her hand and
claimed him. And just that easily, she owned his
heart. "I have horses."

"Good. I like horses," she confided.

"You do, huh?"

The rattle of a cart loaded with lunch trays
sounded outside the door.

"There's your lunch, angel-face," Nikki said
gently. "Let's wash your face and hands."

"I'm not an angel face," Angelica scolded
weakly. "My name is Angelica Rose Petersen."

"Okay, Angelica Rose," Nikki teased gently.
"Whatever you say."

The little girl closed her eyes while Nikki washed
and dried her face, then held out her hands, her
brown eyes fixed gravely on Cully while her sister
performed the same task on her fingers.

"Are you going to give me your bones so I can get better and go home?"

Nikki's fingers froze in the task of folding the towel, her gaze flying to Cully's face. *Trust a child to cut to the heart of the issue.*

"Sure, honey, I'll give you my bones. But I think maybe the doctors have to test me to find out if my blood is good enough for you first. Then, if the test matches, they'll only need a little part out of the middle of my bones."

The smile that curved his mouth and lit his eyes with warmth stole Nikki's breath. This was the Cully she remembered.

"That's right," Angelica agreed solemnly. "They need your bone's middle. Thank you, Cully."

"You're welcome, angel-face," he murmured softly. The lump of emotion in his throat wouldn't allow normal volume.

Behind them, the door whooshed open, letting hallway noises into the room. "Good morning. And how is everyone this morning? Are we ready for lunch?"

Cully gladly gave way to the bustling orderly, moving across the room to lean against the wall by the tall window.

Nikki left the friendly orderly arranging Angelica's wheeled table and tray of food and joined him. "Thank you, Cully."

He glanced down at her. Tears glittered on her thick lashes, her brown eyes carbon copies of her little sister's.

"You're welcome." He shifted, his voice gruff with emotion. "You know that there's no guarantee I can give her my 'bone middle.'"

"I know." Nikki managed a watery smile. "I've told her a dozen times that it's bone marrow, but she keeps calling it 'bone middle.' I think she gets confused because the doctor told her that he takes marrow from the middle of the bone."

A half grin quirked Cully's mouth, quickly disappearing as he looked across the room at Angelica once again.

"Damn. What if Quinn and I don't match?"

Chapter Two

Nikki drew a deep breath, her gaze following his. "Then we keep searching." She looked up at him. "And you won't have to bother with one more illegitimate child making a claim against Charlie's estate."

"Hell." He stared at her, his mouth hard. "I suppose I'm going to have to apologize for that remark."

Startled, Nikki eyed him hesitantly. "Well," she said slowly. "Only if you're sorry for saying it."

"All right, dammit. I'm sorry."

Cully was clearly tired, impatient and reluctant to apologize. Still, he'd said the words.

"What?" he demanded as she continued to eye him silently.

"You. That's the first time I've had someone snarl at the same time he apologized. In fact," she said, "I don't think I've ever heard you apologize before."

"Well, don't expect it to happen very often."

"I won't."

A small smile lit Nikki's face, erasing the weariness, softening the lush curve of her mouth. The urge to touch her cheek and stroke his thumb over the damp lower curve of her lips was so strong that Cully shoved his hands into his back pockets.

"Did you talk to the doctor this morning about blood tests?" he asked, abruptly changing the subject.

"Yes, I did. He wants you to check in at the hospital lab and have your blood drawn as soon as possible. He said he'd tell the technicians to expect you."

"All right. I'll do that. What floor is the lab on?"

"First. If you take the elevator down to the lobby and follow the hallway to the right, you can't miss it."

"Thanks. I'll be back when they're finished with me."

Nikki nodded in response, her gaze following him as he left the room.

An hour later, Cully was back on the fifth floor, a bandage stretched tightly over the small ball of cotton pressed against the vein where the needle had drawn out his blood.

Chatting with a nurse in the hall just outside the closed door to Angelica's room, Nikki glanced up and saw him. A wave of deep relief and appreciation swept her as she noted the proof that he'd given a blood sample.

The nurse's gaze followed Nikki's. Cully halted abruptly when the two women stopped speaking and stared at him.

"Sorry. Am I interrupting?" He half turned to leave, but Nikki caught his sleeve, stopping him.

"No, Cully, don't go. We were just discussing what Angelica can expect from the next step if you're confirmed as a donor."

The nurse's polite smile warmed. "Cully? Are you Cully Bowdrie, Nikki and Angelica's brother?"

"No, I'm not Nikki's brother," Cully shot back.

"But I thought…" The nurse glanced from Cully to Nikki, clearly confused.

"You were wrong," he snarled.

Nikki frowned at Cully, taking pity on the embarrassed nurse. "There's no blood connection between Cully and me. We have different parents. It's only Angelica who may share the same father as Cully."

"Oh. I see. Well…" Visibly taken aback at Cully's hostile denial, the nurse nodded at Nikki. "I have to run. If you have any more questions, please don't hesitate to ask. I've found it's helpful for the patient if the family is familiar with the procedures."

She gave Cully a brief, cautious smile and hurried down the hall.

"Well. You certainly know how to clear the

area.'' Nikki assessed Cully's tense body and the black frown that lowered his brows and thinned his lips. ''I'm relieved that you seem to have our tangled family connections worked out. I was definitely uneasy about the remote possibility that I might be considered your sister.''

''You're not my sister,'' Cully ground out. ''And I damn sure don't feel like your brother.''

Nikki couldn't reply. She was pinned by the raw emotion that blazed in his eyes. His lashes lowered, his gaze moved down her body and back up again in a searing trail that left her pulse racing and her temperature climbing. She couldn't read the underlying emotion in his eyes, but the heat and need was unmistakable. When his gaze returned to hers, she was trapped by the web of sexual energy that pulsed between them.

She'd counted on her anger burning out any remaining shred of desire for him. That he could arouse her with one hot look made her furious.

''Stop it!'' she whispered fiercely. ''Just stop it. I don't want this.''

He didn't pretend he didn't know what she meant. ''Neither do I,'' he said bluntly.

Nikki ignored the shaft of pain that stabbed her chest, and shook her head in frustration. ''Then stop looking at me like that.''

Nikki heard him swear under his breath as she shoved open the door to Angelica's room and walked in, refusing to look back. It wasn't until she reached Angelica's bedside that she realized the little girl was awake, though her eyes were sleepy and nearly half-closed.

"Are you mad at Cully?"

Startled, Nikki forced a reassuring smile, curling her fingers around the child's small hand. "No, sweetheart, I'm not angry with Cully. We were just discussing something."

Angelica wasn't convinced. Her worried gaze went past Nikki's shoulder and focused behind her. "But you *look* mad, Nikki. Are you mad at Nikki, Cully?"

"No, angel-face, I'm not mad at your sister." Cully's deep tones held conviction.

"Good." Angelica accepted his words.

"How's our patient today?" A white-clad nurse bustled into the room, pushing a wheelchair ahead of her. She halted next to the bed and patted the chair's handle grips. "Ready for a trip in your race car?"

"Yes!" Angelica's wan face lit with anticipation.

"Good." The nurse smiled at the two adults. "I'm going to take our little speed demon here downstairs for some tests that the doctor ordered."

"Test? Oh, no, not more tests." Angelica's face clouded. "I don't *want* more tests. Are they going to stick me with needles again?"

The nurse nodded, her face sympathetic. "I'm afraid so, hon. But if you're a good girl and don't cry, I'll stop at the nurses' station and we'll see if we can find you an ice-cream bar when we're done. What do you think?"

Angelica pursed her lips, her expression calculating. "I think we should get one for me and one for Nikki, too."

"Angelica Rose," Nikki warned, smothering a smile. "Don't be greedy."

"I'm not being greedy," she protested. "I think you deserve an ice cream, too." Her gaze flicked to the nurse. "With chocolate on the outside, right? Maybe nuts?"

"Definitely chocolate. I'm not sure about the nuts."

"Okay." Through with bargaining, Angelica turned a satisfied smile on her sister. "And if you can't eat all your ice-cream bar, Nikki, then I'll help."

Nikki rolled her eyes. "I'm sure you will," she said dryly.

The nurse grinned. "Why is it that I have visions of Angelica eating both of these bars?" Her shrewd gaze scanned Nikki's face. "While we're gone, why don't you check out what the cafeteria has to offer for lunch?"

"Thanks, but I'm not hungry," Nikki replied, easing the blanket and sheet to the foot of the metal bed before tucking Angelica into her robe.

"Humph." The nurse set the brakes on the chair. "I bet you didn't eat breakfast, either, did you?"

"I had a piece of Angelica's toast." She eased her sister's legs off the bed and supported the little girl with an arm beneath her elbow as she stood. The nurse did the same with Angelica's other arm.

Together, they gently tucked the child into the chair.

"And I suppose you slept here in that recliner last night, too?"

Nikki shrugged, giving the woman a small smile. "Guilty."

The nurse shook her head in exasperation. "You've been sleeping in that recliner and barely eating ever since your aunt left four days ago. You're going to make yourself sick. Then who's going to look after our little angel here?" She tucked the edges of the robe around Angelica's legs and winked at her, earning a smile before she stood and fixed Nikki with a stern look. "You need to eat and sleep on a regular basis." Her gaze switched to Cully. "You're bigger than she is. Why don't you drag her down to the cafeteria and make her eat something while we're gone?"

Cully's eyes narrowed on Nikki's features. Rebellion was written clearly on her face, and he knew that the moment the motherly nurse cleared the doorway with her charge, Nikki would refuse to go anywhere with him. But the smudges beneath her eyes and the prominence of her cheekbones told him that the nurse was right. Nikki needed to eat. And get more sleep. He wondered how many nights she'd stayed awake watching over Angelica.

"Since I missed breakfast myself, lunch sounds like a good idea. C'mon, Angel, I'll race you to the elevators."

"Okay. Last one there is a horse-apple."

Before Nikki could voice a protest, the nurse set

the wheelchair into motion. Cully's fingers closed over Nikki's elbow, easily subduing her instinctive move to tug her arm free of his grip, and he urged her into motion, the two of them walking close behind the chair.

"Are you coming, Nikki?" Angelica twisted to look behind her, her eyes bright in her thin face beneath the long fall of black hair. "You have to eat. The nurse said."

"Yes."

Angelica and the nurse waited with them until the elevator arrived. A passenger held the door open as the nurse deftly maneuvered Angelica's wheelchair inside but the crowded elevator didn't have any room for Cully and Nikki.

"We'll wait for the next elevator," Nikki said, smiling reassuringly at Angelica. "Enjoy your ice cream."

"I will. Maybe the cafeteria has ice cream so you can have some too."

Nikki laughed. "Maybe."

"Bye." Angelica waved as the doors slid shut, closing her in.

"You can let go of my arm now." Nikki tugged and he released her immediately. She took a step away from him, moving sideways to widen the gap between them. She leveled her gaze at him, meeting his unreadable stare without blinking. "And just for the record, I don't appreciate being manhandled."

He shrugged. "Then I'll feed you instead. You need to eat and get some sleep."

"That's my decision to make. You've been here

less than ten hours, hardly enough time to decide what I need.''

"You've lost weight." His hand cupped her cheek and his thumb brushed the faintly bruised-looking skin beneath her eyes before she jerked away from his touch. "And you have dark circles under your eyes. It doesn't take a genius to see that you're not taking care of yourself."

"I'm perfectly fine," she said stubbornly.

"Sure you are. When was the last time you ate a whole meal, not a piece of Angelica's toast?"

"Last night."

"What did you eat?"

"I had a guest tray and ate with Angelica— chicken, I think, and rice. Not that it's any of your business," she added. His assumption that he had the right to question her about her actions irritated her. But then she clenched her teeth and struggled to remember that she owed him nominal politeness in return for his agreeing to have his blood tested.

"And when was the last time that you ate a meal away from the hospital?"

"I don't know. A few days ago, a week, maybe.''

"Isn't there a decent restaurant at your hotel? Or room service?"

"I cancelled my hotel room yesterday. It was a waste of money. I rarely went there." *Besides, I can't afford it.* Although the foundation paid Angelica's expenses, their largesse didn't extend to family members, and Nikki's modest savings account was being depleted faster than she'd expected.

Cully tensed, searching her features in disbelief. "You mean you never leave the hospital? You've been sleeping in that damn recliner in your sister's room every night?"

"That recliner is perfectly comfortable," she answered, her voice cool.

"Maybe for sitting, but not for sleeping. Hell, no wonder you look exhausted. You're not sleeping at all, are you?"

"Of course I'm sleeping. I'm not—"

The elevator doors opened. A trio of people waiting to board shifted aside to allow them to exit, and Nikki bit off the rest of her reply in midsentence.

Cully half turned toward her, but before he could touch her, Nikki walked quickly out of the elevator.

"The cafeteria is this way." She gestured down the wide hall to their left. He walked beside her, following her as she picked up a tray and joined the queue at the counter. She refused to continue their argument, even when he eyed the mug of tea and the glass of orange juice on her tray and growled something under his breath.

She left him settling his bill with the cashier, and walked across the nearly empty cafeteria to a table against the far wall, where floor-to-ceiling windows looked out on an enclosed courtyard filled with greenery and flowering plants.

She transferred her tea and juice to the table and slipped the tray onto an empty table behind her, staring out at the summer garden. Brilliant pink and deep red blooms glowed against the lush green leaves of rose bushes.

The roses are in full bloom. How long has it been since I've been outside the hospital? More than a week, she realized with dismay. *And longer since I've looked, really looked, at plants and flowers.* It was disquieting to have lost track of normal life. Perhaps the nurses were right. And much as she hated to admit it, perhaps Cully's analysis was correct, also.

Cully slid a plate onto the table in front of her.

"What's this?" she asked.

He set a carton of yogurt and several small plastic containers of hot sauce in front of her. "Enchiladas," he said briefly. He emptied the tray, setting another steaming plate, a carton of milk and a huge slice of apple pie on the table opposite her. He placed the empty tray beside hers on the table behind them before he slid into the chair across from her, dropping his hat onto a third chair at the table and unrolling a knife and fork from a paper napkin.

Unfazed by Nikki's silent stare, he ate at least a quarter of the enchilada on his plate before he looked at her.

"It's good," he said. "You should try it."

Nikki considered dumping the food into his lap. But the steam that drifted up from her plate carried the rich smell of tortillas, beef and spices, and awakened the appetite she'd been so sure didn't exist.

"Forget that I'm the one who gave it to you, Nikki. The nurse has a good point. You can't help your sister if you collapse because you haven't eaten or slept.''

The green gaze fastened on hers was oddly gentle, and though his matter-of-fact tone wasn't coaxing, neither was it demanding.

Both he and Sandra, the motherly nurse, were right, Nikki conceded reluctantly. If she didn't take better care of herself, she might fall apart long before Angelica was ready to go home and take up her normal, little-girl life.

Nikki picked up her fork and took a bite.

Cully covered a sigh of relief by swallowing a gulp of milk. She was so damn slender. When he took her arm earlier, he'd been startled by the fragility of the bones beneath his fingers. The tailored white shirt that she wore tucked into jeans was loose, the crisp cotton shaped by the slope of her shoulders and the rounded curves of her breasts. The jeans were faded as if she'd worn them for some time, but although the denim faithfully followed the shape of her bottom and slim thighs, Cully guessed that the jeans must be at least a size too big.

Touching her had been a mistake, he reflected grimly. It brought back swift, vivid memories of her bare skin, her body satin-smooth beneath his stroking hands, both of them lost in heat and passion.

One night hadn't been nearly enough to satisfy the hunger for her that still smoldered inside him. Not that he planned to do anything about it. He wasn't the same man she'd given herself to four years before. He had nothing to offer Nikki—or any

woman, for that matter. And only a fool would fan
a fire that was likely to burn him alive.

"Thank you, Cully."

He glanced up to find Nikki cradling her tea mug,
the enchilada plate empty.

"Not bad for hospital food, was it?"

"No, not bad at all." Nikki sipped her tea. "I
think it's my turn to apologize."

He lifted his head warily. "For what?"

She sighed and pushed the empty plate aside,
moving the nearly full mug into its place.

"You were right—I need to eat even when I'm
not hungry. Angelica's health is fragile, and if anything happened to me, she'd be all alone in the
hospital."

"Where's your aunt Cora? Why isn't she here
with you?"

"She was, for a while. But her boss needed her
and she had to go back to work."

"Her boss? She's still baking pies for the Crossroads, isn't she?" Cully knew that Colson's Crossroads Grill had established a reputation across half
the state of Montana for their pies and pastries
solely because Cora Petersen had been the Grill's
baker for the last twenty years.

"Yes, she is."

"Couldn't Eddie get someone to take over for
her so she could be here in Denver with you and
your sister?"

"He tried. Bonnie Akins took over for Aunt
Cora, but then her daughter needed her in Missoula
to help with a family emergency of some sort.

Eddie couldn't find anyone else, so he had to call Cora and ask her to come home.''

"She should have quit."

"Not Aunt Cora. She loves her job. She says keeping busy and involved keeps her young."

"Yeah?" Cully nearly offered to pay the equivalent of Cora's salary so she could return to Denver and her grand-nieces. He doubted that Nikki would accept the offer, however. Besides, getting involved with Nikki and her family any more than he already was just wasn't a good idea.

"Yes." Nikki sipped her tea, watching through lowered lashes as Cully finished eating. The sleeves of his pale yellow shirt were folded back, leaving his forearms bare. Suntanned skin was dusted with fine black hair, a heavy silver watchband with a chunky, utilitarian face glinting against his dark skin. One hand cupped his coffee mug, the sight eliciting a flash of memory of those same square-tipped fingers and that callused palm moving over her body with heart-stopping sensuality, stealing her breath. Each brush against her sensitized skin had fed the heat that threatened to consume her....

He lifted his cup, his hand moving out of her line of vision. Shaken, she forced herself to focus on downing the last sip of tea and setting the mug carefully down on the table before glancing at her watch.

"I think I'll go back upstairs. Angelica's tests should be finished by now, and she frets and worries if she's alone in the room and I'm away too long." She pushed her chair back and stood.

"Is that why you sleep in her room every night?" Cully asked, collecting his hat and rising to follow her.

"Yes."

"Are you sure it's only because Angelica worries?" Cully followed as she left the cafeteria, noisy with the late lunch crowd, and started down the hall to the elevator. "Or because you worry about her when you're away?"

"Probably both," Nikki admitted with a shrug. She glanced sideways at him and found him settling the Stetson on his head, tugging the brim down over his forehead. She'd seen him perform that small task dozens of times in the past, and the familiar gesture underlined a deep sense of loss. The resulting wave of pain was so strong that she caught her breath. With an effort, she tore her gaze away from his profile and focused on speaking evenly. "Force of habit, I suppose. I've been more mother than sister to Angelica ever since our mom died."

"How old was she when you lost your mother?"

"Fourteen months."

Which would have made Nikki around seventeen, Cully calculated swiftly. No wonder she felt such an overwhelming sense of responsibility for her little sister. Nikki was probably the closest thing to a mother Angelica had, except for their aunt Cora. But Cora Petersen had to be in her late sixties, he thought, so it made sense that the little girl had turned to her older sister for mothering.

They rode the elevator upward in silence, and

found Angelica back in her bed, her long lashes dark fans against her cheeks as she slept peacefully.

Nikki crossed quickly to the bed and bent over the little girl, brushing a strand of black silk from her temple. Cully followed more slowly, struck by the poignant, telling gesture.

The phone rang, the sound startlingly loud in the hushed room. Nikki moved to answer before it could ring again and wake Angelica, but Cully stopped her.

"I'll get it."

He strode past her and picked up the receiver. "Hello." He paused briefly, listening. "Yeah, this is Cully. I got in late last night."

The call was clearly for him, but Nikki couldn't help overhearing his end of the conversation in the quiet room. He stood on the far side of the bed, half turned away from her as he spoke, his gaze focused out the window on the blue skies and bright sunshine of another hot summer day.

"I don't know. The lab drew blood this morning, but it will be at least a week, maybe two, before we know the results." He was silent, a frown growing as he listened to the party on the other end of the line. "Can't Quinn handle it?" He bit off a curse, glancing at Nikki and the sleeping child. "All right, I'm on my way. But I'll leave my truck here, fly home and call from the airport in Wolf Point when I get in. You'll need to drive down or send Ed to pick me up." He listened briefly. "Right. See you."

He hung up the phone and swung to face Nikki.

"You're leaving?"

"Yes." He gestured dismissively. "Business problem. Normally Quinn would handle it while I'm gone, but he took Victoria and little Sarah camping, and can't be reached for a few days. I'll be back as soon as the situation is resolved or Quinn is home and can take over."

"I see." Nikki didn't understand the disappointment and sense of loss that she felt. She hadn't wanted him here, and now that he'd donated blood for testing, surely his departure was a welcome relief. Still, the sharp twist of distress remained.

He crossed the room and stood beside her, looking down at Angelica, sound asleep and unaware of the tension between the two adults.

"I don't want to wake her." His voice was quiet, purposely lower so as not to disturb the child. "Will you tell her goodbye for me when she wakes?"

"Of course." Nikki's gaze left Angelica's pale face and settled on the man next to her. His shirtsleeve brushed her bare arm, the warmth of his big body heating the small space that separated them, making her feel the impact of his presence as if he touched her from shoulder to thigh. He was silent, his hard face brooding as he stared down at the sleeping little girl.

"She'll ask me if you're coming back. What shall I tell her?" Nikki knew that it wasn't only Angelica who would want to know when, and if, Cully would be returning. Still, she kept her voice as noncommittal as possible.

He flicked her a sideways glance, green eyes nearly hidden behind lowered black lashes.

"I don't know. I'm not sure how long it will take to get the problem sorted out." He took a pen and business card from his shirt pocket, scribbled on the back of the card and handed it to her. "This is my home phone number. If you need me, leave a message on the machine. I told the lab to call and let me know the results of the blood tests at that number, so I'll check it every day."

"All right." Nikki closed her fingers over the card. His gaze narrowed on hers, his features hard and unreadable.

"Are you going to be all right here by yourself?" he asked abruptly.

"Of course." Surprised, Nikki frowned. "Why wouldn't I be?"

"For one thing, you can't seem to remember to eat regularly. And for another, you don't seem to think that you need to sleep in order to function."

Nikki's chin firmed. "I told you in the cafeteria that I'll eat."

"And what about sleeping?" he demanded. "Are you going to keep spending your nights sitting in the recliner, watching Angelica?"

"I'll ask the nurse for a cot," she conceded, reminding herself that he was cooperating with blood testing and that the least she could do was rein in her urge to tell him that her sleep, or lack of it, was absolutely none of his business. That her welfare was not his concern and that she didn't appreciate the inference that she needed him to monitor her sleeping and eating. Still, she couldn't keep the edge of irritation from her voice. The quick flash of matching irritation that moved across his face told her that he'd read her mood accurately.

"Good. Make sure you use it."

Nikki bit off the sharp reply that trembled on her tongue, and refused to answer.

"I'll be in touch," he said when it became obvious that she didn't mean to respond.

Nikki nodded. Cully stared down at her for one long moment, his green gaze intent, before he touched his fingertips to the brim of his Stetson and strode abruptly from the room.

"Men," she muttered, releasing her held breath in an audible expulsion. Her heart was beating too fast, and now that she was breathing again, she realized that Cully's presence seemed to have sucked all of the oxygen from the room. She refused to consider that a long, searing glance from Cully had caused the trip-hammer beat of her pulse.

Three days later, just before lunch, Cora Petersen walked into Angelica's hospital room.

"Hello, girls."

"Aunt Cora!" Nikki's cry of surprise echoed Angelica's delight. "What are you doing here? How did you get here? How long can you stay?" Their words tumbled one over the other.

Cora's eyes twinkled as she returned Nikki's warm hug. Then she bent over the bed to receive an equally enthusiastic hello from Angelica, while she answered their questions in order. "I'm here to keep both of you company, I flew from Montana on a plane, and I can stay as long as I want.''

''But what about your job? I thought Eddie couldn't find a replacement?'' Nikki perched on the end of Angelica's bed while Cora settled into the comfortable bedside chair.

''He couldn't,'' Cora said. ''Cully Bowdrie brought in a pastry chef from Great Falls and told Eddie he'd guarantee that she'll stay until I'm ready to come back to work. Eddie fussed and fretted, but he finally gave in.''

''Oh.'' Nikki was stunned.

''I must say, I thought it was mighty nice of Cully,'' Cora commented, her shrewd gaze trained on Nikki's face. ''But I can't help wondering how he knew that I needed a replacement. Not to mention the hotel.''

''Hotel?''

Cora took a sheet of paper from her purse.

''A hotel room has been reserved in our name, all expenses paid by Bowdrie Brothers, Inc., for as long as we need it.'' She handed the paper to Nikki.

Nikki read the brief typed note. ''Why would he do this?'' she murmured aloud.

''I don't know, but I'm certainly glad that he did,'' Cora said firmly. ''Did you notice the address of the hotel? It's only a few blocks from this hospital, which means that it's close enough for us to walk back and forth.''

''Yes, I see.'' Her aunt was clearly delighted by Cully's arrangements, but Nikki had an uneasy feeling that there was more to his generosity than was obvious at first glance. He was a Bowdrie. Rich and powerful, the two brothers were accustomed to getting their own way, regardless of whom they were dealing with. Though his intervention on Cora's behalf was certainly kind, Nikki couldn't help but worry that it was also a hint of what they might expect from the Bowdries if Angelica proved to be related to them.

Everyone in Colson knew that the Bowdries took care of their own—whether it was a brother, land, cattle, horses or dogs. How much more possessive would they be of a little half sister?

Nikki was uneasy about accepting Cully's largesse, but she couldn't tell Cora how she felt. Not when Cora and Angelica were so delighted. Nikki didn't even want to consider the cost of the hotel, because she had no idea how she would ever repay him. To be honest, she was overwhelmingly grateful that Cora was here to share the emotional stress of dealing with Angelica's health.

She only wished that she didn't have Cully Bowdrie to thank for her aunt's presence.

Ten days later, tears brimmed, trembling on her lashes before spilling over to trail unnoticed down her face as Nikki dialed the phone number Cully had written on the back of his business card.

"Yeah."

The brusque male voice startled her. She'd expected to get an answering machine and leave a message, not reach Cully in person.

"Hello, Cully. This is Nikki."

"What's wrong?"

"Nothing. Nothing's wrong—in fact, something is very right." She drew a deep breath, steadying her voice. "The doctor was just here. He told me that the results of your blood tests are back. You're a match, Cully."

Silence echoed over the phone line that connected them.

"We match?" Cully struggled to come to grips with her words. "My blood matches Angelica's? Then she really is my half sister."

"Yes," Nikki agreed.

"I'll be damned." He breathed the words aloud as he thrust his unsteady fingers through his hair, raking it back off his forehead. "I never really thought there was a snowball's chance in hell that we'd match. When Quinn told me that you claimed Charlie fathered Angelica, it sounded too implausible. What's the likelihood that we had a sister in Colson that Charlie didn't know about?" He broke off, then added doubtfully, "Or did he? Did Charlie know before he died that Angelica was his?"

"I don't think so. As I told you, my mother told Aunt Cora about the baby's father when Angelica was born, but mentioned Charlie to Cora only that one time. As far as we know, she never told anyone else."

"Why not?"

"I don't know. She and Aunt Cora didn't care for your stepmother. Maybe she was afraid that Charlie would want visitation rights and she'd have to deal with Eileen. Or maybe she simply didn't want the town to know that she'd had an affair with a married man." Nikki shook her head. "I don't know, Cully. I'm as much in the dark about my mother's motives as you are."

"If Charlie had known about Angelica, he would have claimed her." Cully's words were filled with conviction. Nikki stiffened warily.

"I'm sure that my mother wouldn't have kept Charlie from seeing Angelica," she said carefully. "But neither would she have wanted Charlie to interfere with her upbringing."

"Angelica is a Bowdrie," he said flatly, "and Bowdries take care of their own. Dad would have provided for her while he was living as well as after he was gone. And since he isn't here to do it, Quinn and I will look after her interests."

Nikki's fingers curled into fists. "Angelica is being looked after just fine. She doesn't need you to take over her life."

"You mean you don't want me involved in her life," Cully said grimly.

"No. That's not what I mean. I mean that I don't want you taking over Angelica's life. She's accustomed to me and to Aunt Cora—being cared for and disciplined by us. We don't have a lot of money, Cully, but she's always been loved and safe with us. I don't want that security shaken for her—certainly not now. Not when she's ill and her whole life has been turned upside down."

Silence stretched tautly over the telephone line. "All right," he conceded at last. "I'll back off—for the moment. But at some point, you're going to have to deal with the fact that she's not just yours anymore, Nikki. Quinn and I have just as much right to claim her as you do.''

''I'm not saying that you can't have a place in her life, Cully, only that the time isn't right for us to argue about what role you'll play.''

''Hell, I don't see what there is to argue about,'' he muttered darkly. ''You're acting like you think we'll sue you for custody.''

Nikki stiffened, drawing in one swift breath in a faint but audible gasp.

''I'll be damned,'' he said softly. ''You do think I'd try to take her away from you, don't you?''

''I didn't say that.''

''You didn't have to. I can hear it in your voice.''

Chapter Three

Nikki couldn't deny his accusation. She *was* worried about what Cully and Quinn might expect of her small family and how those expectations would change their lives. The Bowdries had a lot more money and power than the Petersens. There was no question that if Cully wanted to sue for custody, there was a very good chance he would win.

Her silence spoke volumes to Cully.

"I didn't think it was possible for anyone to think I'm a bigger bastard than I do myself," he said bitterly. "I guess I was wrong."

"Cully, I don't think you're—"

"No." He cut her off. "Don't lie. I've never given you any reason to think any better of me." He drew a deep breath, ignoring the pain in his chest. "I'd better check in with the doctor. Thanks for calling with the test results. I appreciate it."

The line went dead. Nikki pressed the receiver to her forehead, eyes closed.

He sounded so bitter.

She couldn't deny that she didn't trust him not to take over Angelica's life. She knew that his loyalty and commitment to his brother went bone deep, and she instinctively knew that he would extend that fierce protectiveness to Angelica. While Cully had a reputation for being a hard man, he was also respected for being honest and straightforward.

He had to have known that I was in love with him four years ago, despite the fact that neither of us ever said the words, she reflected with painful honesty. *Which only proves that he didn't love me, or he would have extended that same powerful commitment and protectiveness to include me. And he wouldn't have married someone else and broken my heart.*

That he had made love with her one unforgettable night, only to marry someone else days later, cut her to the bone. That she was forced to let him back into her life because of Angelica was impossibly difficult.

Yet somehow, she had to find a way to survive his presence in her life.

I know that I'll have to share Angelica's time and affection in the future, she admitted to herself starkly. *And sharing her is a small price to pay for the miracle that Cully is able to donate bone marrow. But exactly how I'm going to handle dealing*

*with Cully on an ongoing basis is another matter
entirely. I don't know how I'll manage.*

"Damn!" she muttered as she let the receiver
drop back into its cradle. "Now I suppose it's my
turn to apologize."

Three days later, Nikki left the visitors' waiting
area down the hall from Angelica's room, balancing
a paper cup of coffee in each hand. She glanced up,
halting abruptly when the elevator doors slid open
and Cully stepped in front of her.

"You're back." She knew the flat statement held
no welcome. She couldn't help it. He stirred conflicting emotions in her, and she deeply resented the
swift surge of pleasure that warred with the ever
present anger and bitter sense of betrayal.

"Yeah." He gestured toward Angelica's room.
"How's she doing?"

Nikki glanced down the hallway, her stomach
clenching with worry. "Chemotherapy is tough,"
she said honestly. "She's suffering from severe
nausea. And her hair began falling out in big
clumps so I had to cut it all off. She's a real trooper,
even when she's nauseated, but she cried when she
lost her hair."

"Damn." Cully's fingers closed over the brim of
his hat, crumpling the edge in his fist. He forced
his fingers to unclench. "Giving her medicine that
makes her sicker sounds so damned backwards."

"I know. I agree." Nikki read his frustration in
the muscle that ticked in his jawline and the grim

set of his features. "But her own bone marrow has to be destroyed before they can transplant yours."

"I know." Cully thrust his fingers through his hair and settled the hat on his head, tugging it lower over his brow. "I understand the theory. I just don't like it."

"Neither do I," Nikki agreed. "And Angelica doesn't, either." She turned to lead the way down the hall. "Although to be honest, she's more accepting than I am." She paused outside the doorway to the room and glanced up at him. "She's determined to get through this so she can get well and climb on one of Quinn's horses. Or one of yours—she doesn't care which."

A quick grin curved Cully's mouth, his eyes warming with amusement. "Remind me to tell Quinn about that. His daughter is a charmer, but stubborn as a little mule. Maybe offering her rides on a horse would get her to cooperate."

"I've found that bribery is almost always useful when dealing with Angelica," Nikki commented dryly, moving toward the door. "Though I try to use it only as a last resort."

"I'll see if I can remember that."

Nikki halted. "I should warn you that she's definitely weaker than the last time you saw her. And she's self-conscious about her hair."

"All right." His gaze met hers as she turned to face him. "Relax, Nikki. I'll try not to let her know that I'm worried."

His deep voice was gentle. His understanding caught Nikki unprepared, and she blinked back quick tears while she attempted to swallow past the lump of emotion blocking her throat. It was unsettling to feel grateful for his empathy. She was much more comfortable with the anger that had accompanied every thought of him for the last several years.

Cully reached over her shoulder to push open the door, and for a moment she felt surrounded by his heat and solid bulk. Oddly comforted by the sense of support, she frowned at him, confused by her reaction. Finding comfort from this man was the last thing she'd expected. His searching gaze met hers for a long moment before his lashes swept lower, narrowing his eyes and making it impossible for her to read his expression.

"After you," he said politely.

Nikki moved past him into the room. Cora was seated in a chair next to the bed, her fingers busy with knitting needles and a partially stitched, blue wool sweater on her lap. She looked up as Nikki entered and a smile broke over her lined face.

"There you are, Nikki. And Cully! How nice to see you."

"Afternoon, Miss Petersen."

"Hi, Aunt Cora. Is Angelica asleep?"

"Nope," Angelica responded, peeking out from behind the book lying open on her pillow. "I'm not taking a nap until we read the next chapter."

"Ahh, I see." She pretended not to notice that Angelica was hiding from Cully behind the open book. Nikki placed the coffee cups on a cabinet and

pointed to a stack of hospital gowns and masks next
to the sink just inside the door.

"Angelica is extremely vulnerable to germs right
now, so all visitors have to wear these," she explained when Cully looked at the blue hospital
gown in confusion. "And we need to wash our
hands, also."

He nodded in understanding, turning away to remove his hat and place it on a shelf above the small
coat rack. Nikki was vividly aware of him waiting
silently behind her while she scrubbed her hands.
She made short work of the task, stepping aside to
let Cully take her place at the sink, and quickly
donned her own gown and mask before collecting
the two cups of coffee and delivering one to her
aunt.

Cora slipped the lid from the cup, eased her
white mask below her chin, inhaled the steam, and
sighed with appreciation. "I have to admit, one
thing I miss about working in the kitchen at the
Crossroads is that I always had a fresh pot of coffee
at my elbow," she commented. "And for goodness
sakes, Cully," she chided as he joined them, "call
me Cora." She pushed herself up and out of the
chair and waved her knitting at the vacant seat. "Sit
down and visit with Angelica for a few minutes
while I walk down the hall a bit. My bones ache if
I sit in one place for too long."

"Yes, ma'am," Cully answered, but his gaze
was on the slender child propped up in the bed,
peering at him from around the edge of the hard-
cover book. A floppy hat covered her head, its soft

brim framing her face. She was thinner, the bones of her face sharper beneath their covering of pale skin. In contrast, her eyes seemed bigger, the irises an even darker brown.

"Hey, Angelica, how are you doing?"

"Quite well, thank you." Her words were precise, her expression solemn. "But the chemotherapy made me sick to my tummy, really sick."

"That's what I heard from your sister. Pretty nasty stuff, huh?"

Angelica rolled her eyes and grimaced in disgust. "Yes. *Very* nasty." Distracted by the conversation, she abandoned the shelter of her book and leaned forward to whisper confidingly, "I threw up so many times that I lost count, and even Nikki couldn't remember the number. Yuk, gross."

Cully nodded in commiseration. "Sounds pretty gross, all right. But it won't be too long before you're finished with the chemo treatments, right?"

"Yup. And the doctors don't give chemo to donors, only to recipients, so you don't have to worry, Cully." She patted his hand comfortingly before she fixed him with an intent, solemn stare. "We're so lucky that we found you, Cully. After we found out that Nikki and I didn't match, Dr. Harris said that it might take months before we found a donor because people who aren't related only have a one in five thousand chance of having identical blood types. So you see, you're my own special miracle." She beamed at him. "I absolutely believe in miracles, don't you?"

"Uh, yeah." Cully's stunned gaze moved from

Angelica's smile to Nikki's guilt-stricken features. *She hadn't told Angelica that he was her brother?* Of course she hadn't, he realized grimly. She looked guilty as hell.

"I want a miracle like the little boy in *The Secret Garden.*" Angelica chattered on, demanding Cully's attention. He tried to focus on her conversation.

"The boy in the garden?" He didn't have a clue what Angelica was talking about, and his brain was having a difficult time getting past the fact that his little sister still had no idea that they shared more than compatible blood.

"You know, *The Secret Garden.*" Angelica lifted the book from her lap and held it up so he could read the cover. "Nikki and I are reading it— it's one of our favorite books. We love books about gardens. We Petersens are gardening women, you know." The last comment was quoted in a near-perfect imitation of Cora's voice and inflection. "Didn't your mother read it to you when you were a little boy?" Her voice returned to a child's curiosity.

"No, she didn't." Cully didn't tell her that he couldn't remember his mother, that she had left when he was far too young to even remember what she looked like. Nor did he tell her that no one had ever read a book to him in his entire life. Her delight and pleasure in the activity were completely foreign to him.

"Oh, that's too bad." Her gaze fastened on

Cully, filled with sympathy that lightened as a smile grew. "I know! You can read it with us, okay?"

"Well, I don't know…" Cully began.

"Oh, yes. It will be just perfect." She clapped her hands, her words spilling over his in quick delight. "We've just started, so you won't have missed much of the story at all, and I can tell you all about the part that we've already heard, okay?"

Cully didn't have the heart to deny her. "Okay."

"Great." She beamed at him. "I just know we're going to be best friends, aren't we?"

"Uh, sure." He cleared his throat and awkwardly patted the little hand that clasped his forearm.

"Oh, we will, I'm ab-so-lute-ly sure." She drew out the syllables in exaggerated emphasis. "Now, let me tell you about the beginning of the story, and then you can read the next chapter out loud, okay?"

"Okay." The kid was a miniature steamroller, he thought, as she launched into an animated description of the events he'd missed in the first two chapters of the book. She was clearly crazy about the story, throwing in side comments about how much she liked the little girl and how cranky the little boy was because he was ill. By the time Angelica was finished, Cully's head was reeling with overload.

"And now you can read chapter three and we can see what happens next," Angelica announced at last, handing him the book with an air of conferring a great honor.

"Angelica, maybe Cully doesn't want to read aloud," Nikki suggested.

"I don't mind." He took the book from Angelica and scanned the cover, then looked back at Nikki. "Reading is as good a way as any to pass the time, and since I'll be here for a few days, maybe I'll find out how the story ends. And maybe you'll have time to explain the 'secrets,' Nikki."

His stern expression told her that he was angry she hadn't told Angelica he was her half brother. Nikki knew he deserved an explanation, but she had no intention of giving him one while Angelica listened. "Maybe. We'll have to discuss those— later."

"Tonight."

His voice was inflexible. Nikki's gaze flicked to Angelica's confused frown before returning to Cully. "All right. Later tonight."

"But Nikki, you shouldn't tell Cully all the secrets from the book. Won't that spoil the story for him?"

Nikki managed a smile for the puzzled little girl. "No, honey, I don't think so. You've read the story more than once and knowing the 'secrets' doesn't mean that you don't still enjoy the story, does it?"

"No," Angelica said slowly. Her expression said that she still wasn't sure the adults were right.

Cully distracted her. "Okay, so where do I start reading? What page?"

She leaned closer, small fingers opening the book and turning pages until she reached a bookmark with a grinning green frog. "Right here, right at the beginning of the new chapter, see?"

"Right." Cully settled into the chair and began to read.

It was ten o'clock that evening before Angelica fell asleep for the night.

Cora settled into the comfortable recliner with her knitting, a cream-colored wool afghan tucked over her legs. "You should go to the hotel, Nikki, and try to get some sleep. You, too, Cully. Don't you have to start your physical exams tomorrow?"

"Yes." Cully nodded. "I check in at 7:00 a.m."

"Then you'd both better scoot."

"Are you sure you wouldn't like me to stay with Angelica tonight, Aunt Cora?" Nikki asked.

"No, I'm perfectly comfortable. I have my knitting and a good book." Cora made a shooing gesture. "Off with you. Tomorrow night I'll go to the hotel and you can stay."

"My truck is parked downstairs. I'll give you a lift to the hotel."

"All right." Nikki gave in to the inevitable. She had to talk to Cully sometime, and the short ride to the hotel would guarantee that the argument she was sure they were going to have wouldn't last long.

They were silent on the ride down in the elevator. Cully held the lobby door for her, following her out into the dark night. She hesitated at the sidewalk and he gestured toward the left.

"The truck's this way, about half a block."

The air was heavy, thick with electricity, the

moon obscured by rolling dark storm clouds that threatened rain.

Wind gusted, skeining Nikki's hair across her face and throat. She ducked her head, her fingers catching her hair to tuck the long strands behind her ear. Cully's hard fingers closed around her elbow, and she struggled to keep up with his long strides as they hurried down the sidewalk to the truck. He unlocked the passenger door and yanked it open, catching her waist to swing her up into the cab.

Nikki didn't have time to protest before the door slammed behind her. Seconds later, the driver's door opened and he slid beneath the wheel, closing the door on the growing storm outside and shutting them into the relative quiet of the cab. The door had barely clicked shut when the dark skies opened and rain pelted down, drumming against the metal roof.

"Just in time," she murmured, her gaze on the stream of water pouring over the windshield.

"Yeah." He twisted the key in the ignition and the engine turned over with a rumble.

The tension in the air was palpable. Nikki braced herself, deciding that the sooner she faced his anger, the sooner the inevitable confrontation would be over.

"Cully, about Angelica..." she began.

"This isn't a conversation we can finish in the five minute drive to your hotel." He looked at her, one swift encompassing glance, before he shifted the truck into gear. "Fasten your seat belt."

He eased his foot off the clutch and the big truck began to move. Nikki snapped her seat belt into place and stared out the windshield as he drove the few blocks between the hospital and her hotel. The drumming of raindrops on the roof and the rhythmic swish of the windshield wipers were the only sounds that broke the taut silence.

Cully wheeled the truck into a parking space just beyond the hotel entrance. It took only moments for him to hurry Nikki out of the truck, across the wet sidewalk and through the revolving doors into the lobby.

The quick dash from truck to hotel through the falling rain had dampened her unbuttoned cardigan and the front of her blouse. Nikki brushed at her sleeves and wiped droplets of moisture from her cheeks and lashes while they waited for the elevator.

Even through the cotton sweater that separated her skin from his, Nikki felt the press of each individual fingertip where Cully's hand circled her arm. Her nerves tingled with awareness. Warmth spread from her biceps through the rest of her body, chasing away the slight chill from the damp rain and replacing it with heat. She tugged gently in an effort to free herself from his touch, but Cully's grip only tightened. She glanced up at him. He stared straight ahead, his profile austere.

"You can let go of me," she said quietly. "I don't plan to run away."

His gaze snapped from the elevator to her face.

Nikki's instinctive step backward from the anger in his eyes was halted by his grip on her arm.

"Maybe you need to be reminded that I'm not going away until we have a talk. Just in case you change your mind about running."

His voice was quiet, but the cord of steel running beneath the grimly polite words made her shiver. She realized that she was unconsciously straining against his hand, and abruptly forced her muscles to relax.

The elevator pinged, the doors sliding open to let a group of chattering guests exit. Nikki and Cully waited silently, letting the crowd flow past them, before stepping into the empty elevator. Cully released her arm and leaned forward.

"Our room is on the—"

Cully pushed the button for the eighth floor before Nikki finished her sentence.

"How did you know that my room is on the eighth floor?" Nikki spoke without thinking.

"Because I made the reservation," he said flatly.

How could she have forgotten his kindness in arranging for the room for herself and Cora?

Nikki was silent as they rode the elevator upward, then walked down the hall to her room. It was really a compact suite, with a small living area, a tiny kitchen-bar, two bedrooms and a bath.

"I'm going to make some coffee," she announced as she concentrated on fitting the key into the lock. Dealing with Cully was something she had to learn to handle. Angelica was tied to him by blood, and because she loved her little sister, Nikki knew that contact between herself and Cully was unavoidable. Their lives would be far easier if she could maintain an atmosphere of civility. "Would you like some?"

"Sure." He followed her into the room.

Nikki was painfully aware that they were alone together for the first time in four years. She moved away, needing to put some distance between them, and gestured toward the sofa and upholstered chair that created a cozy conversation area near the window. "Have a seat. I'll only be a minute."

But he didn't sit. Instead, he prowled across the room, dropped his hat on a small table next to the sofa and stared broodingly out the window.

Nikki stole sidelong glances at him as she poured water in the small coffeemaker and measured coffee into the basket. By the time she collected mugs from the small overhead cabinet and located sugar packets, Cully had paced back across the room. He crossed his arms on his chest and propped one shoulder against the wall, his gaze intent on her as she poured coffee into mugs.

"Why didn't you tell her?"

His harsh demand startled her. Nikki jerked, splashing drops of coffee onto the countertop before she recovered. "Because I thought she had enough to handle at the moment, and I don't want her upset."

"You think she'll be upset to learn that she's related to the Bowdries?"

Cully didn't move away from the wall, but his

big body tensed, muscles flexing in response. Nikki could feel anger coming off him in waves.

"I didn't mean that I think Angelica would be disturbed or unhappy to learn that you and Quinn are her brothers," Nikki said carefully. She met his narrow-eyed stare and handed him the steaming mug. "I only meant that I believe it would be better to tell her when she's got less on her mind. The bone marrow transplant may save her life, but it also means more drugs and treatment for possible rejection. All of this is pretty overwhelming for the adults around her, and she's just a little girl. How much more difficult must it be for her to cope?"

"All right. I agree that she doesn't need any more bad news," he conceded. "But if you think Angelica would be happy to know she has brothers, why wouldn't that be good for her?"

"Because it radically changes the makeup of her family, and her life has already undergone too many catastrophic changes. I don't believe more change of any kind is good for her right now."

"I disagree," he retorted. "I think knowing that her family has expanded and she has more people who care about her would make her feel safer. And I think she should be told the truth."

Nikki drew a deep breath. Unfortunately, she recognized all too well the stubborn set of his chin. "And I can't agree. I don't think now is the time to tell her."

"Just when *do* you think would be the right time to tell her?"

"I'm not sure. Perhaps after the transplant procedure."

"I'm beginning to think that you're the one who isn't ready to deal with being connected to the Bowdries."

Nikki's fingers gripped the mug tighter. Heat moved up her throat, warming her cheeks, but she refused to look away from the accusation in his eyes. "I admit I'm concerned about the impact you'll have on all our lives, Cully."

His eyes narrowed over her. "Just what, exactly, do you think I'm going to do to you, Nikki?"

Break my heart again. The thought came swiftly, unbidden, but she didn't want him to know that she was still so vulnerable to him.

"I don't know, Cully," she prevaricated. "And that's what bothers me."

"You don't know? That's it?" He set his coffee mug down on the counter with a clunk. "That's not a good enough reason. She's my sister and I don't plan to stay out of her life until you decide it's time to tell her we're related."

"I need to focus on what's best for Angelica." Nikki stood her ground, refusing to be intimidated. "There's no question that suddenly adding two males to our family of females is going to make a difference."

"Well, hell yes, it's going to make a difference. You'll have family to teach Angelica to ride horses and help with homework, to fix the kitchen sink if a pipe breaks or change the oil in your car." Cully waved a hand, impatient and frustrated. "What's wrong with having a little help when you need it?"

"There isn't anything wrong with any of those things, Cully. In fact, it all sounds great. But who decides how late she can stay up on a weeknight, or what her punishment is if she breaks a rule?" Nikki was beginning to get frustrated at his inability to see her view. "And if you want to buy her an expensive toy that I don't think she should have, how do we decide if she gets it or not?"

He stared at her for a long moment.

"I see." His eyes slowly darkened to deep emerald. "The real issue is whether or not we can cooperate with each other and be good parents."

The question shot straight to her heart. Nikki nodded, unable to speak, struggling to block out the memory of the dreams she'd once had of Cully and a child of their own.

His gaze grew darker, his lashes lowering as he searched her face.

"She's a great kid, Nikki. You've already proved that you can be a good mother. I can't blame you for worrying about whether I'll be a good influence in her life, but I promise you I'll do my best." He pushed away from the wall and took one slow, measured step toward her. "I'd never do anything to hurt her. But I don't have any experience with little eight-year-old girls, so you'll have to tell me if I do something that you don't think is right for her." He lifted his hand, trailing his fingertips gently over the silky arch of her eyebrow before cupping her cheek in his palm. "I just want you to share her with me, Nikki. Can you do that?"

His voice was husky and deep, his work-roughened palm warm where it cradled her cheek. His fingertips made small, stroking movements against her skin. Nikki shivered, taut with indecision. Her intellect told her to move away from him, but her senses urged her to stay.

"I, uh..." Nikki lost her train of thought when his thumb brushed over her lower lip. "I'll try, Cully, but I don't know if..."

"Shh." His fingertip against her lips stopped her words. "That's all I'm asking."

Nikki stared at him, worry and indecision tormenting her.

"Stop worrying," he commanded, his voice gravelly. He rubbed his fingertip lightly between her brows, smoothing out the frown that creased the soft skin. "It's going to be all right."

Then he bent closer, replacing his fingertip with his lips. Nikki's lashes drifted lower as she breathed in the scent of his aftershave. His lips traced her eyebrows, then the outward curve of her cheekbone, finding the soft skin beneath her ear. Nikki caught her breath, mesmerized by the nearly unbearable pleasure.

This isn't smart, Bowdrie, Cully's conscience whispered.

He'd only meant to reassure her, only wanted to ease the vulnerable uncertainty so easy to read in her eyes. But the feel of her warm, soft skin under his lips lured him closer, tempted him to test the curve of her cheek, the fragrant tender skin just below her ear.

She moaned, a soft, breathy sigh. Cully might have listened to his conscience, might have had the strength to pull away, but then her body swayed toward his, and the warning voice inside his head was drowned by the roar of desperate need.

He slipped an arm around her waist, supporting her as her knees gave way and she rested lightly against him, her hands still clutched around her mug, which was pressing against his midriff. His mouth couldn't bear to leave the soft heat of her skin as he eased the mug from her unresisting hold and set it blindly on the counter before reaching for her again. He threaded his fingers through her hair, cradled her head in his palm, and his mouth found hers.

Her arms wrapped around his waist, her hands grasping his shirt to pull him closer. A wave of fierce satisfaction swept Cully as he realized that she wanted this, wanted him, as desperately as he wanted her.

Outside in the hallway, a group of hotel guests erupted from the room across the hall. Their chatter and laughter intruded on the hot silence that cocooned Cully and Nikki, breaking the spell that held them.

Cully froze, struggling to reclaim his balance. Still immersed in passion, Nikki murmured against his lips, protesting the loss when he lifted his head.

He forced his muscles to move, sliding his arms

from around her in slow motion until his hands came to rest on her waist.

"No." Her muttered word was barely audible, but he eased a step back, distancing their bodies. His brain knew he needed to break contact, but separation was painful. Every cell in his body cried out in protest at the loss, demanding that he lock her lush curves against him again. When her arms slipped from around him, her fingers giving up their grip on his back, Cully nearly gave in to temptation. "This was a mistake," he managed to say, his voice hushed. He removed his hands from her waist, curling them into fists at his side, hoping that she hadn't noticed the fine tremor that shook them.

It didn't help that her eyes were dazed and dark with emotion, her mouth faintly swollen from the pressure of his. He wanted to touch her, to smooth his lips over the damp curve of hers, to trace the silky angles of her face. He wanted to lose himself in her. His desperation was so sharp that he knew he had to get out of the room before he gave in to the need to strip her naked and lift her onto the counter beside them.

He was so attuned to her emotions that he felt the shift in the air between them, knew the instant that passion cleared from her brain and she realized what had happened. Her chocolate eyes flared with shock, then narrowed and darkened with anger, her slim frame going poker-stiff, her chin tilting with outraged pride.

"I told you I didn't want this," she said. Anger pulsed in the air between them.

"And I told you that I didn't want it, either," he answered shortly. "But what's between us isn't going to go away just because neither of us wants it."

"I think you should leave." Her voice shook with emotion.

"I think you're right." But his feet didn't move. Her diamond-bright gaze held his unwaveringly. He wondered uneasily if that brightness came from tears. He hoped not. "I'm sorry."

The words were curt, shorter than he'd meant them to be, but dammit, if she cried, he'd be on his knees. *Please, baby, don't cry.*

"So am I."

And that said it all, he thought grimly.

He retrieved his hat and pulled open the door to the hall. He paused, glancing back at her. She stood in the dimly lit kitchenette just as he'd left her, chin up, her fathomless gaze fixed on him. "Good night."

"Good night." Her reply was cool. It didn't encourage him to linger. As he rode the elevator up to the tenth floor to his own room, he wondered if she knew that he was booked into the same hotel. If she did, she wouldn't be happy, he reflected.

Later that night, unable to sleep, tortured by hot dreams and too-vivid memories of how she'd felt in his arms, Cully fervently wished that he didn't know Nikki was sleeping only two floors down and mere minutes away from him.

He knew that he'd crossed too many bridges to ever go back to her. Any hope of a future with

Nikki had been destroyed the day he'd agreed to marry Marguerite.

He wished he could as easily kill the stubborn part of his heart that refused to stop loving her, regardless of what he'd done, regardless of what she believed he'd done.

Grimly, he forced himself to concentrate on the only thing he could allow to be important: Angelica.

Chapter Four

Nikki held herself perfectly still, joints locked in place, for a long time after the door closed and Cully disappeared. Then her knees gave way and she sagged, catching herself with a hand braced against the cabinet.

Oh, no. She groaned, closing her eyes in a vain effort to shut out that last image of him as he looked back at her from the doorway. Trying to erase the memories of the press of his body against hers, of his mouth on hers, was just as impossible. *I can't let him do this to me again. I won't care about him. I won't let myself love him. I won't believe his promises.*

But a small voice inside her head told her that it

was too late, and much as she tried to deny it, she had the feeling that the prediction was true.

Determinedly, she unplugged the coffeemaker, snapped off the lights and went through her bedtime preparations on automatic pilot. Sleep eluded her, however, and the moments spent in Cully's arms replayed themselves over and over in her dreams, leaving her frustrated and restless.

The impact of those all-too-brief moments was devastating. For four years she'd worked hard to forget Cully Bowdrie and lock away the dreams she'd once had of love, marriage and a family with him. She'd believed that she'd succeeded and moved on with her life, left with only a residual anger that flared on occasion. It had taken only a few moments to prove to her that she'd lied to herself. It wasn't anger that had urged her to hold him, that had opened her mouth to his with eager abandon, that had made her want to cry out in protest when he stepped away from her.

She wanted him. Badly. And nothing she'd done, nothing she'd told herself in the last four years, had changed that fact one iota.

Her eyes gritty from lack of sleep, Nikki walked into Angelica's room the following morning and halted abruptly. A strange nurse was bent over the bed, tucking the sheet more closely about her patient. Wondering briefly if she'd entered the wrong room, Nikki shifted for a better angle and verified that her little sister was the child asleep beneath the smooth sheet.

"Good morning." Nikki's voice was little more than a whisper.

The nurse glanced over her shoulder and nodded in greeting, then adjusted the sheet once more and left the bed to approach Nikki.

"Hello. Can I help you?"

"I'm Nikki Petersen, Angelica's older sister. I don't believe I've seen you before. Are you new to pediatrics?"

"Oh, Miss Petersen. I'm glad to meet you." The woman's smile lit her plain face. "I'm Dana Phillips. Mr. Bowdrie hired me to provide private nursing care for Angelica while she's here in Denver."

"I see. I'm afraid Mr. Bowdrie didn't tell me that he was employing a private nurse." Nikki glanced at Angelica once more. "How long has she been sleeping?"

"Only a few moments."

"I won't disturb her then. Have you seen Mr. Bowdrie this morning?"

"He was here earlier, but he left about five or ten minutes ago. I believe he said he was going down to the gift shop to look for a magazine and then stop at the cafeteria for coffee."

"Thank you." Nikki crossed the room and brushed a kiss against Angelica's brow. The little girl was indeed sleeping, and her eyelids didn't so much as flicker at the soft touch. "I'll be back soon," Nikki murmured to Nurse Phillips as she crossed the room and quietly opened the door to the hall.

She caught the elevator to the lobby floor and met Cully just as he left the gift shop.

"I need to talk to you."

"All right." He halted, his gaze unreadable.

Nikki glanced around them at the crowded, noisy lobby area, but found no spot that wasn't busy. "Not here."

Cully's gaze followed hers, scanning the huge room. "How about the cafeteria? I'll buy you a cup of coffee."

"No." Nikki's voice held an edge that revealed the anger she was trying to contain. "Let's go outside to the garden." She leveled her gaze on him. "If I raise my voice outside, I'm less likely to disturb anyone."

Cully lifted a brow. "You plan on yelling at me?"

"No, I do not plan to yell at you," Nikki said with exaggerated politeness. "But the possibility always exists whenever I'm forced to discuss anything with you."

His response was a wry half smile.

Neither of them spoke until they reached the garden. Then Cully waved her to a seat on a bench in the shade of a Japanese maple and sat on the other end, his forearms propped on his thighs. He turned his head and looked at her. "Well, what have I done this time?"

"You hired a private nurse for Angelica without discussing it with me."

Her accusation clearly startled him. He stared at her for a moment, a puzzled frown drawing his dark brows into a V. "You don't want her to have good nursing care?"

"Of course I want her to have good care! I want her to have the best care possible. That's not the point. You should have discussed it with me before you hired a nurse."

"Why?"

Nikki could feel her temperature rising. "Why? How can you ask me why?"

"Easy. Because I don't have a clue why you're so damned upset. If you want Angelica to have the best care possible, then why the hell would you mind if she has a private nurse?"

Nikki drew in a deep, exasperated breath and slowly exhaled in an effort to keep from raising her voice. "Because the decision is one that my aunt and I should have shared with you. Because you aren't the only concerned relative Angelica has. Because you've only been involved with her for a short time, while either Aunt Cora or I have raised her for the last eight years! Because..." Her voice had grown increasingly louder. Nikki drew another deep breath and purposely hushed her tone. "I don't want to scream at you, Cully, but you can be *so* dense."

"So the real reason you're so ticked off is not because of what I did, but because I didn't talk with you before I did it?"

"Yes. Brilliant deduction, Sherlock."

"Would you have told me not to hire the nurse?"

"No, of course not. But that's not the point."

"I think that's exactly the point. If the roles were

reversed and you were the one who had the means to hire a private nurse, would you have talked to me first?''

"Yes, I would have. You're a man accustomed to control, Cully. I don't want you taking over Angelica.''

His eyes narrowed, anger turning them a darker green.

"This isn't about me controlling Angelica. This is about you not wanting me involved with her.''

"That's not true.''

"Yes. It is,'' he said flatly. "Once I donate the bone marrow, you'd just as soon I disappear, admit it.''

"You'll walk away from Angelica sooner or later. Better now than later, before she's attached to you and grows to depend on you.''

"Where the hell did you get that idea? I told you I want to be involved in her life.''

"I know what you said. But you don't do long-term relationships, Cully.''

His mouth thinned and a muscle flexed along his jawline. "If you're trying to get rid of me, Nikki, you're backing a lost cause. If I'd known that she was my sister, I would have been involved in her life since the day she was born. And I damn sure plan to be involved from now on, whether you want me to or not. Get used to it.''

He rose in one lithe movement and loomed over her, a brooding figure radiating anger. Refusing to be intimidated, Nikki stood and met his hot glare.

"And before you accuse me of trying to control

anybody, Nikki, you'd better take a hard look at yourself. This isn't about Angelica. This is about what happened between us four years ago.''

''That's not true.''

''No? Then let's ask Cora how she feels about Angelica having the best nursing care I could find. I'm willing to bet that she'll be relieved.''

Nikki's lips compressed. She was furious, but she couldn't argue with his claim. Cora was desperately glad that the Bowdries had taken an active interest in Angelica's plight.

''Cora doesn't know you like I do, and she only sees the benefit to Angelica now, not the damage you can do to her down the road.''

''Well, maybe you should listen to your aunt. Because it seems to me that unless we all focus on what's best for Angelica right here, right now, there won't be a 'down the road' for her.''

Nikki had no response, no argument to refute his assertion.

''All right,'' she said stiffly. ''I agree that each moment is important for Angelica right now.'' She paused, cataloguing the anger that tensed his big frame and curled his fingers into fists at his side. ''But so help me, Cully, if you hurt her...''

Her voice trailed off, the fierce, unvoiced threat hanging in the air between them. He glared at her for long moments before the tension eased from his body and the fierce emerald gaze fixed on hers lost its intensity.

''Sometimes things aren't what they seem, Nikki,'' he said obliquely. ''And sometimes a man has no choice about what he does." He tugged his ever-present Stetson lower over his brow, shading his eyes. "I can't promise you that I'll never disappoint Angelica, but I promise you that I'll never purposely do anything to hurt her."

"All right."

He stared at her for a long moment, but Nikki couldn't give him any more encouragement. She didn't trust him not to hurt Angelica because she was sure that after the current emergency was over and they were all back in Colson, he would get on with his life and be too busy to spend time with his half sister. Nikki was also sure that it would break Angelica's heart, for she'd never had a strong male influence in her life and she'd taken to Cully instantly, claiming him as her own.

Just like I did, Nikki thought painfully. *And look how much damage he did to me.*

Cully's mouth tightened when she said nothing further. With an abrupt nod, he turned and walked away from her, striding across the manicured lawn and disappearing inside the hospital.

Nikki sat abruptly, the angry adrenaline that had fueled her moments before draining away and leaving her legs curiously unsteady.

Much as she hated to admit he was right in any possible way, Nikki knew that Cully was half-correct when he'd accused her of reacting to him now based on their prior relationship. She wasn't using Angelica to punish him for her failed dreams of having a family with him. But the core of her concern about his relationship with Angelica did stem from her knowledge of just how badly her own failed dreams had hurt her. She didn't want Angelica damaged in the same way, and she was determined to prevent it.

The meditation garden was peaceful and quiet, soothing to Nikki's troubled thoughts. She stayed on the bench, shaded from the hot sun by the maple's leafy canopy, breathing in the scent of roses and alyssum and the earthy smell of fresh-turned dirt in the flower beds.

One of the doors leading to the hospital corridor opened and closed, the sound distracting her from the aged gardener as he clipped the shrubs against the far wall.

"Nikki!"

She glanced over her shoulder, a smile growing as she recognized Victoria Bowdrie and her husband, Quinn.

"Hello, you two. I wasn't expecting you—what a nice surprise."

"No, don't get up." Victoria dropped onto the wood-and-cast-iron bench next to Nikki and tugged her husband down beside her. "Ahh, this is nice." She glanced around, appreciation written on her face as she scanned the shady greenery and brilliant blooms. The sun gleamed off beautifully tended flowers. "What a lovely spot."

"I love this garden." Nikki glanced at Victoria and grinned. "Actually, I love any garden, as you know, but I especially love this one."

"I don't blame you. It's a wonderful contrast to the hospital's sterile chrome and steel, isn't it?"

"Yes, it is." The two women exchanged a glance of complete accord. "What brings you two to Denver?"

Nikki didn't miss the quick look Victoria shared with her husband.

"Something important came up and Quinn needs to discuss it with Cully."

Something about the way Victoria spoke and the concern in the look she gave Quinn sent a shiver of worry streaking up Nikki's spine.

"Does it have anything to do with the transplant?" She tried to keep her anxiety from her voice, but knew she failed.

"No," Quinn answered. "Not at all. Just some business that I need to discuss with Cully in person."

"Oh, I see." Nikki had the feeling that there was more to this than Quinn was saying, but he clearly didn't want to elaborate, so she let the subject drop. "Have you seen Angelica yet?"

"Yes. We stopped there first. The nurse said that Cully was at the lab, so we thought we'd look for you. Cora told us that we might find you here."

Nikki glanced at her watch. "Speaking of Cora, I should get back to the room so she can have a break." She stood, brushing a bit of grass from her long, gauzy skirt, her gaze sweeping the peaceful oasis. "She enjoys this garden as much as I do."

"I'm not surprised," Victoria commented. "She's quite a gardener herself. Ever since Quinn and I were married and I gave up my apartment next door, I've missed seeing her flower beds every day. Didn't you miss gardening with Cora when you moved to Seattle?''

"Yes, I did. Of course, I missed my family and good friends like you, Victoria, the most. But I was surprised at how much I missed gardening. I not only missed the flowers, I even missed weeding the vegetable patch.'' Nikki laughed.

"How have you managed to live in a Seattle apartment with no room for a garden?" Quinn asked as he stood, catching Victoria's hand to tug her to her feet.

"I have a patio with pots of herbs and greens,'' Nikki said. "And flowers in hanging baskets. Where there's a will, there's a way,'' she commented wryly.

"Who's tending them while you're away?'' Victoria asked. Hand in hand, she and Quinn walked with Nikki across the grass.

"I have a terrific neighbor—an older woman. She loves the salad greens and herbs I give her, so she was more than willing to water and prune my plants until I get back.''

The trio moved down the brick path toward the hospital doors. "So you're planning to return to Seattle?'' Victoria asked.

"Not anymore, although that was my original plan. When Cora first called to tell me Angelica was ill, the doctors still hadn't diagnosed her illness. I took a leave of absence, asked Emmaline to care for my plants, and flew home, intending to return when Angelica was well. Once the doctors explained how seriously ill she is and how long her recovery period will be, however, I had to rethink my plans.'' Nikki tucked her hands into the pockets of her skirt. ''I know I won't be returning to Seattle. I just haven't had time to make arrangements to close up the apartment and have my things shipped home.''

''So you're moving back to Colson?'' Victoria asked.

''Yes. At least for the foreseeable future.''

''Well, I, for one, will be delighted to have you back in town.'' Victoria caught Nikki close in a quick, hard hug. ''I've missed you.''

''I've missed you, too.'' Nikki returned the hug with warmth.

''And I've missed your cooking at the Crossroads,'' Quinn said as he pulled open the door, winking at Nikki as she passed.

''I thought you were a waitress at the Crossroads?'' Victoria said.

''I was. But when the Grill wasn't busy, Joe used to let me experiment in the kitchen. If Quinn and Cully happened to be there, they were always willing to be my guinea pigs.''

''More than willing,'' Quinn commented as they walked down the hall to the elevators. ''We started timing our arrival to the Grill's slowest time in the hope that we'd be there when Nikki was trying something new.''

''You two were great for my ego,'' Nikki commented fondly. ''You never once refused to eat one of my concoctions.''

''That's because they all tasted great.''

Nikki rolled her eyes in disbelief. Quinn's eyes twinkled, but he didn't back down. "It's the truth, I swear." He held up his hand, palm out, his expression suitably solemn. "Of course, the alternative was to stay home and eat our own cooking, which was pretty bad."

The elevator glided to a stop, the doors opening with a musical ping. Cully was in the room when they reached it, and Quinn drew him outside to talk privately.

Whatever subject Quinn shared with his brother resulted in a new grimness in Cully that disappeared only when he was playing with Angelica. He and Nikki both tried to maintain a truce for Angelica's sake, but the tension between them grew stronger by the day, until Nikki thought she would snap from the strain.

At last, Angelica's team of doctors declared her ready for transplant. The following two days were an exhausting blend of intense moments and painfully slow hours in a countdown to the harvesting of Cully's bone marrow and the transplant to Angelica. And when the actual procedure began, the minutes dragged even more, crawling by for the family gathered in the waiting room. The quartet, made up of Nikki, Cora, Quinn and Victoria, alternately paced or stared at an unending series of news reports on television, while downing cup after cup of black coffee.

At last it was over. The smiling surgeon reported a successful procedure, and the waiting family drew a collective sigh of relief.

Later that night, after Angelica was sound asleep, and nearly an hour after Cora nodded off to sleep, tucked beneath the blanket on a small cot, Nikki gave in to the overwhelming need to see Cully. She'd listened closely as the doctor confirmed that he had gone through the bone marrow removal without difficulty. She understood that, barring any unexpected complications, he would be released from the hospital in twenty-four to forty-eight hours. Still, she felt a compelling need to see for herself that he was okay.

The elevators were deserted, the hospital hallways quiet as Nikki made her way down to the third floor. The woman at the nurses' station in Cully's section seemed familiar, and Nikki realized that she'd shared a dinner table with the woman in the crowded hospital cafeteria only two days before. The white-clad nurse looked up from her paperwork, smiled and nodded when Nikki told her where she was going.

Moments later, Nikki eased open the door to Cully's room and slipped inside.

The room was lit by one small, shaded light on the wall just inside the door. Nikki moved quietly across the shadowed room to the bed. Cully was asleep, his short-sleeved, white hospital gown a stark contrast against his sun-darkened skin. The sheet and blanket were pulled up to his waist, and one arm was lying against his pillow with the palm up. A narrow cable, attached to a small rubber cap that covered the index finger of his right hand, was connected to a nearby monitor, its digital readout glowing green in the dimness.

Nikki leaned against the bed rail, her fingers curled over the round metal rung. Cully's lashes were dark fans against his suntanned skin, his mouth relaxed in sleep. Uncombed, his black hair fell across his brow.

Without considering her actions, she brushed the lock back off his forehead, her fingertips lingering in the soft thickness. His hair was cool beneath her fingers, his skin warm. She traced the curve of his brow, the pulse at his temple, the high arch of his cheekbone and the line of his jaw—roughened by the shadow of dark beard—before smoothing her fingers down the proud bridge of his nose. Her fingertip found the indentation between nose and upper lip. Slightly parted, his lips were warm and dry, his breath soft across the tips of her fingers as she followed the bow of his upper lip to the full lower curve of his mouth.

She felt dampness on the back of her hand and realized that she was crying—a slow, steady welling of tears trailing down, cheek to chin, before splashing against her hand.

Seeing Cully like this was devastating. He was vulnerable in sleep—the fierce heat of his eyes hidden behind lowered lashes, the hard line of his mouth softened. Watching this Cully made it easy to remember the charming, easygoing cowboy who had stolen her heart.

Before he'd walked back into her life, she'd convinced herself that she'd moved beyond the love she'd felt for him. Now she couldn't deny that her conviction had been shaken in the past few weeks, even though she knew that nurturing hope for a future with Cully held only a guarantee of heartbreak.

He muttered in his sleep, his forehead pleating in a frown, and he moved restlessly.

Nikki caught her breath, unable to understand his mumbled words, afraid she'd woken him. But his eyelids didn't lift. Instead, the frown deepened.

"Let go of the wheel. Don't..." He jerked, his legs shifting beneath the covers, his voice hoarse and barely audible.

"Cully." Nikki touched his forearm in a light caress. "Cully, wake up. You're dreaming," she said softly.

"Too much blood," he muttered. "Can't stop the blood." His hand fisted against the pillow, the arm muscles beneath Nikki's fingers bunched, his head twisting against the pillow.

"Cully." Nikki bent over him, her free hand stroking lightly over his brow. "Cully, wake up."

He tensed beneath her hands, then opened his eyes and stared up at her.

Nikki froze. There was no recognition in his dark green eyes, only desolation.

"Cully? What is it? What's wrong?"

Awareness replaced the bleak emotion in his eyes. His brow furrowed and his gaze left hers to scan the room.

"Nikki?"

His voice was a rusty whisper, faintly slurred,

and Nikki read confusion in his eyes when his gaze returned to hers once again. Familiar with the effect of painkillers and other drugs on Angelica, she recognized the symptoms.

"I'm here," she reassured him, her fingers gentle as she smoothed his hair back off his forehead. "I'm here, Cully."

"Don't go," he muttered. He caught her hand, threading his fingers through hers and cradling her hand against his chest. "Stay."

"I will."

His eyelids drifted closed, the taut muscles of his big body relaxing, the tenseness fading from his expression as he dropped back into sleep. His grip on her hand didn't loosen, however, and Nikki felt behind her with her free hand until she found the armrest of the bedside chair. She pulled it closer until she could ease into the seat without losing contact with Cully, intending to stay only long enough to be sure that he wouldn't waken. But the warmth of his hand wrapped around hers not only eased Cully's restlessness, it somehow calmed the ache in her own heart. Sometime during the long dark hours before dawn, Nikki fell asleep in the chair, her head pillowed on her arm, her hand in his. When he stirred, she woke to murmur soothingly until he calmed, and they both fell back to sleep, reassured that they were together.

It wasn't until dawn arrived and the quiet outside the room gave way to the morning sounds of a new shift of nurses that Nikki woke. Disoriented, she pushed her hair out of her eyes, wincing as cramped muscles protested the movement. Pinpricks of feeling returned, painfully driving out the numbness caused by hours spent in one position.

Nikki turned her head, the hospital sheet cool beneath her cheek, and looked at Cully. His eyes were open, his gaze fastened on her. Stunned, Nikki was silent, caught by the heated emotion roiling in his eyes.

"I thought I dreamed of you," he murmured. He lifted his free hand and brushed a lock of hair from her cheek, tucking it behind her ear. "You stayed." The simple words carried a wealth of emotion.

"You asked me to."

"Did I?"

"Yes."

Their whispered words carried none of the antagonism and wariness that had marked each conversation they'd shared since he'd first walked into Angelica's hospital room. Nikki nearly wept at the intimate warmth that wrapped them together. This was what she'd missed, she realized. Not just the nearly unbearable heights of making love with him, but this deep connection that she'd shared with no one but Cully.

Behind her, the unmistakable sound of the hallway door opening intruded, letting in the busy world outside and destroying the magic that spun between them.

Nikki pushed herself upright, tugging gently on her hand and Cully let her go, his fingers sliding reluctantly away from hers.

"Good morning." A young orderly entered,

crossing the room to open the drapes. "How are you feeling this morning?"

"Not bad."

Cully's gaze didn't leave Nikki's, but his eyelids lowered and she could no longer read his expression. The abrupt change from connection to cool distance was so sharp that she flinched.

"I'd better go," she murmured, glancing sideways at the orderly. "The doctor's releasing you today, isn't he?"

"That's what he told me, unless there were complications. Except for a little soreness, I feel fine."

"That's wonderful." She hesitated by his bed. "You'll come up to say goodbye to Angelica, won't you?"

He gazed at her for a long moment. "Sure," he said, finally. "I wouldn't leave without saying goodbye."

"Good. That's good." She forced herself to take a step away from him. "Well, I'll see you then."

"All right."

As surely as if his hand were touching her, she felt his gaze between her shoulder blades until she stepped outside the room and out of his sight.

True to his word, Cully appeared in Angelica's room later that afternoon, patiently going through the necessary procedures to enter the room. Angelica's immune system was so suppressed by the chemotherapy she'd undergone before the transplant that she was at constant risk of infection.

He seems pale. Nikki's worried gaze studied him

as he bent over Angelica's bed. *And he's favoring his right leg.*

His usual loose-limbed stride was marred by a slight limp, and Nikki assumed that the doctor must have extracted the bone marrow from his right hip. She frowned, concerned when he lowered himself into the bedside chair and carefully stretched his right leg out in front of him. Reluctant to interrupt his conversation with Angelica, she pretended to read her book while she shamelessly eavesdropped.

"Did it hurt?" Angelica asked, her brown eyes alight with curiosity.

"Nope, I didn't feel a thing," Cully replied. "They wheeled me into the operating room, told me to count backward from a hundred, and I made it to ninety-five. After that, I don't remember a thing until I woke up back in my room."

"Wow." Angelica inched closer to peer over the edge of the bed. "Will you have a scar?"

"I already have a scar," he teased her, tilting up his chin and pointing to the jagged white line that marred the left side of his throat. He hadn't missed the paleness of her face, nor the exhaustion that was clear as she struggled to raise herself before she fell back onto her pillow.

"I know." Angelica waved her hand in a dismissive gesture. "But will you have a *new* one?"

Cully stared at her, clearly taken aback by her offhand dismissal of the mark that he was so conscious of. "Uh, maybe a little one."

"Oh." Clearly disappointed, Angelica's gaze returned to his throat. "That's too bad. Scars are cool. Where did you get that one?"

"Ahh...in a car accident."

"Where?"

"Near Colson."

"Ooh." She contemplated him for a moment. "I bet it really hurt, huh?"

"Yeah. It really hurt."

"Angelica, it isn't polite to ask such personal questions," Nikki interjected.

"I don't mind." As he said the words, Cully realized that for the first time, he didn't feel self-conscious about the ugly scar. Adults often stared and then averted their gaze. It was refreshing to deal with Angelica's frank, uncomplicated curiosity. "Besides, we're connected, right, angel-eyes? You've got my blood cells."

"Right." Angelica grinned at him, a subdued version of her usual beaming smile. "We're blood connected now. We match."

Nikki hardly heard Angelica's pleased confirmation. She was too busy dealing with the unmistakable message that lay beneath Cully's words and in the direct green stare that held hers. The meaning was clear. He hadn't budged from his stand that Angelica should immediately be told that they shared a father.

Gone was the brief, warm connection that had bound them in the early morning. Nikki could have wept at the loss of intimacy even as she acknowledged that the hostility that lay between them was less dangerous to her heart.

She pulled her gaze from his and focused on Angelica. "Nevertheless," she said firmly, "you should have asked Cully if he minded discussing a personal issue."

"But Cully doesn't mind if I ask him questions," Angelica protested.

"I know he doesn't," Nikki said patiently. Angelica's little face was pale, her eyelids heavy with fatigue from the nausea that had plagued her since the transplant. The urge to indulge her was strong, but she and Cora had discussed setting limits with her doctor, and Nikki knew that it was better for Angelica that the adults around her maintain their usual authority and enforced the usual rules. "But you should always ask first, because practicing good manners is important."

"Okay."

Nikki glanced at Cully. He scowled at her, clearly not approving. Belatedly, she realized that he hadn't been present during the discussion with Angelica's doctor, and probably thought she was being unkind.

Darn. I'll have to get him alone and explain why after Angelica is asleep.

She was reluctant to talk to Cully alone, but she'd given him her word that she would do her best to share Angelica with him. And that meant sharing the reasons for the mild discipline.

"Maybe Cully would like to read the next chapter in *The Secret Garden* aloud to you," she suggested in an attempt to distract both Cully and Angelica. Both wore disgruntled expressions that lightened at her words, and she breathed a sigh of relief.

Cully began the chapter, but before he'd read more than a few pages, Angelica was nauseous once more. Nikki quickly produced a metal pan and he took it from her, holding Angelica while she was miserably sick, then washing her pale face and hands with a gentle touch.

Angelica was exhausted by the effort. Nikki silently took the soiled pan and moved away from the bed. Cully trailed his forefinger down Angelica's wan cheek and smiled at her.

"I'm going to leave now so you can get some rest."

"Are you going home?" she asked, the corners of her mouth turning down with sad acceptance.

"Not home to Montana—just back to the hotel." He tapped her lightly on the tip of her little nose. "You're not getting rid of me that easily. I'll be back to see you in the morning, okay?"

"Okay," she murmured drowsily.

Her eyelids drifted lower, to fan against delicate skin.

He was halfway to the door when Nikki stopped him. He glanced down at the slender hand that clasped his bare arm. The warmth from her fingers sent a swift surge of heat racing through his veins. He pulled his gaze away and looked at her.

"What?" The word was too abrupt, his voice raspy with the effort it took to keep from covering her hand with his and pulling her closer.

"Can I talk to you for a minute? Out in the hall?" she whispered.

She glanced at the bed where Angelica lay sleeping and he nodded. "Sure."

Her hand left his arm and a part of him breathed a sigh of relief, while another part mourned the loss of the connection.

They stepped into the hall, the door easing quietly shut behind them. Except for the murmur of voices from the nurses' station at the end of the hall, they were alone, the hallway that stretched away on each side of them deserted.

"I wanted to explain to you why I was firm with Angelica when she quizzed you," Nikki began, determined not to let her reluctance to deal with Cully prevent her from being fair. His accusation in the garden that she purposely tried to cut him out of Angelica's life for her own personal reasons had hit home.

He frowned, his eyes narrowing. Nikki crossed her arms over her chest in an unconsciously defensive gesture. The movement snugged her scoop-necked T-shirt tighter, the white cotton outlining the shape of her breasts with bold accuracy. Cully's pulse hummed a little faster, a little stronger. He tried to ignore his body's reaction and focus on her words.

"I told you I didn't mind answering her questions."

"I know. It wasn't that she was so far out of line, but her doctor talked to Aunt Cora and me about maintaining as normal an atmosphere with her as possible. He explained that when a child is seriously ill, the parents have a tendency to give in to them, to indulge them in both big ways and small. But the child already feels out of control because of the disease, so they desperately need the adults to calmly maintain order and set parameters. That sense of normalcy makes them feel safe."

"Are you telling me that you lectured her about good manners because that's what you would normally do if she weren't sick?"

"Yes. Although I wanted to let her keep asking you questions for the rest of the day if they kept her mind off how sick she is."

"I thought she was doing well?" Cully's gaze sharpened with apprehension.

"She is," Nikki hastened to assure him. "The nausea she's feeling is a perfectly normal reaction to the transplant. And one of the least dangerous reactions she could have."

"Let's hope it's the only reaction she has," Cully said grimly.

"Yes. I pray constantly that she won't develop complications."

"You think that'll help?" He'd been standing too long in one position and his hip ached. He shifted his weight in a vain attempt at relief.

"Of course. Don't you?"

He doubted anyone would pay attention to a prayer from a man like him, but from Nikki? He'd never known a woman as honest and good as Nikki. So maybe she had a shot.

"If you believe it will help, then you should do it."

"But you don't." It wasn't a question.

"No, I don't think heaven's likely to listen to any request from me."

"Why not?"

"I've got my reasons."

And he wasn't going to share them with her, Nikki realized. He was willing to discuss Angelica, but his shuttered expression was as clear as if he'd posted a No Trespassing sign.

"Well…" She gestured at the room behind them. "I should get back inside, in case Angelica wakes. I promised I wouldn't leave her while Aunt Cora went back to the hotel to shower and change."

"Right." Cully nodded. "I'd better get going. I'll see you tomorrow."

His words reminded her of his comment to Angelica. "You told Angelica that you weren't going home to Montana tomorrow?"

"No. I'm staying."

"You're staying?" She stared up at him. "For how long?"

He shrugged. "For a while. Work is slow at the moment and whatever needs doing, Quinn can look after. I'm staying until I'm sure Angelica is going to be okay."

"Oh. I see." Nikki was stunned. She hadn't expected him to remain in Denver, hadn't thought past the transplant.

Cully waited a moment, expecting a protest from her or at least further comment, but she only stared at him without speaking, her brown eyes wide with dismay.

"Why are you so surprised?" he asked bluntly. "I told you that I planned to be involved in Angelica's life. Did you expect me to go back to Montana as soon as the transplant was completed?"

"Yes." Nikki nodded her head slowly. "That's exactly what I expected. The doctors can't tell us how long it will be before Angelica can be released. It depends on how well she accepts the new bone marrow. She may be able to go home fairly soon, or it could be months. How long do you plan to stay?"

"I don't know." Cully shrugged. "As long as it takes, or until something comes up that Quinn can't handle for me. Do you have a problem with that?" The words carried an edge.

"I'm sure Angelica will be delighted that you're here." Dazed, Nikki avoided answering his question.

"That makes one person who's glad I'm sticking around." He glanced at the closed door to Angelica's room. "You'd better get back to her." He tugged his Stetson lower on his brow. "I'll see you tomorrow."

Nikki wasn't sure if his words were a promise or a threat.

"Fine. I'll tell Angelica."

He nodded and walked away. Nikki watched him stride down the hall to the elevator before she pushed open the door and entered the quiet room. Angelica slept peacefully, unaware of her sister's conflicted thoughts.

Chapter Five

Nikki busied herself throughout the remainder of the day and evening with dozens of small chores, some designed to keep Angelica occupied and content, most intended to keep her own mind occupied.

But when evening arrived, after Angelica had taken her medication and fallen asleep, and Cora had returned to the hotel for a night's rest, Nikki found sleep elusive.

Tucked into the comfortable cot, Cora's beautifully knitted afghan covering her legs, Nikki could no longer hold back thoughts of Cully's stunning announcement earlier in the day.

Standing beside his bed in the hushed darkness the night before, watching him sleep, had torn down the walls she'd erected so carefully around her heart. She wasn't at all sure how she would cope with seeing him every day. And for how long? He'd admitted that even he didn't know how long he would stay in Denver.

Outside the hospital window, a three-quarter moon floated high in the black vault of the night sky, sending a shaft of cool light through the window to fall across the blue wool covering her legs. Nikki stared out the window at the pale moon, her gaze unfocused as she gave in to the flood of memories of a cherished friendship that had unexpectedly exploded and turned her and Cully into lovers one incredible, devastating night.

She loved dancing with Cully. Slow dancing, her head against his shoulder, his arms wrapped around her waist, her fingers buried in the silky thickness of his hair just above his nape.

They'd danced together often on the crowded floor at the Crossroads Bar, but tonight was different. This was the first time they'd been alone, in the privacy of a home instead of surrounded by people on a public dance floor. Nikki had hoped this would happen when she volunteered to apartment-sit for a vacationing friend. The reality was better than her dreams.

The living room windows were pushed open, the night breeze gathering the scent of sweet alyssum from the flower beds below and bearing it upward to the second-floor apartment. Mixed with it was the fragrance of sage from the buttes and pastures beyond Colson's city limits. The stereo in the cor-

*ner played one slow, dreamy song after another.
The lamp next to the sofa was turned down low and
created a dim circle of light that barely reached
beyond the table it rested on.*

*Nikki turned her cheek, tucking her face into the
warm curve of Cully's throat. His arms tightened,
pressing her closer until their bodies were sealed
together, her breasts crushed against his chest,
their thighs aligned. Their steps slowed until they
barely moved, swaying to the music. Cully's hands
moved restlessly over her nape to her waist and the
curve of her hip before he cupped her bottom, lifting her onto her toes until the soft cove of her hips
fitted intimately against his. The surge of need that
pounded through Nikki's veins stole the air from
her lungs until she could barely breathe. She
opened her mouth against the hot skin of his throat
and felt his pulse beat more swiftly under her
tongue. His arms contracted and his body tensed.*

*"Nikki," he muttered, his voice thick. "I should
go."*

*Instinctively, her arms tightened and she clung to
him. "No." She tipped her head back to look up at
him, forcing eyes that felt leaden to focus. "Don't
go. Stay."*

*He stopped swaying to the music but he didn't
release her. Encouraged, Nikki brushed openmouthed kisses against his throat, then the underside of his chin. His eyes, already heavy-lidded,
were green fire beneath thick lashes, his gaze fastened intently on her. Nikki flexed her fingers*

against his scalp, urging him to lower his lips to hers.

His mouth took hers and she was lost. Her eyes drifted shut, her world narrowing to the slow, drugging movements of his lips against hers and the press of his much bigger, harder body. The kiss grew hotter, the force of it pressing her head back against his shoulder. His hand cradled her cheek, holding her still for the slow thrust of his tongue.

Nearly frantic with the need to get closer, she arched against him, drowning in the growing fever that sent a river of fire rushing through her veins.

His hand left her cheek, slipped under her loose top and closed over the curve of her breast.

She caught her breath, her body stunned with the swift surge of heightened arousal. Shuddering, she tore her mouth from his and buried her face against his throat. His cheek rested against her temple, his breath harsh in her ears. Her breasts grew heavier, and her nipples tightened almost painfully in an agony of anticipation.

And then his hand moved, his palm cupping the weight of her breast while his fingers stroked over the upper curve, the nipple nudging his palm.

Because of the summer heat, she wasn't wearing a bra. His callused fingers were faintly rough against her bare skin, a reminder of their difference, male and female.

"Baby, tell me to stop."

The words were guttural. Nikki was drowning in pleasure and completely incapable of stopping him, even if she'd wanted to. Instead, she opened her mouth against his throat again, delicately licking the hot, slightly salty skin. He groaned and caught her mouth in a swift, wet kiss that left her shaking, then he leaned away from her just long enough to pull the short cotton top up and off. Nikki barely had time to realize that her torso was bare before he bent and kissed the tip of her breast. Her fingers clenched in his hair, shock urging her to protest, but then his mouth closed over her nipple and the wet heat and tugging suction made her knees buckle.

Instead of pushing him away, her hands pulled him closer. The world narrowed to his mouth on her breast and the press of his body against hers. Gone was the living room with its shadowed lamps. Even the slow beat of the music faded beneath the roar of her pulse in her ears.

Every tug of his mouth, every press of his tongue against her ultrasensitive breast sent a river of sensation straight through her. She wanted, needed something more. What that was, she didn't know, but she knew that she had to be closer to him. She twisted against him, but it wasn't enough. Frustrated with the restrictions of clothes and the difference in their heights, she wrapped her leg around his and pushed herself higher. He responded by groaning what sounded like a curse, catching her bare knee in one hand, carrying her a few steps and pinning her flat against a wall. Then he lifted her, his hand sliding up her bare thigh to curve over her bottom.

"Wrap your legs around my waist."

She immediately complied and sighed with relief when the movement pressed the notch of her thighs against his rock-hard length. He inhaled sharply, his fingers closing over the round curve of her bottom. Vaguely aware that he'd gone still and that she should ask him why, Nikki couldn't stop the overpowering demand of her body. She rubbed against him, nearly sobbing with the intense stab of pure relief.

He reacted by wrapping both arms around her bottom and nearly crushing her against the wall, his body surging against hers in several powerful strokes before he froze, shuddering with the effort. Then he pulled back and, with her in his arms, strode down the hall. Dazed by passion and arousal, her arms and legs wrapped around him, Nikki barely knew that they were moving before she was on her back on the bed. Cully peeled off her skirt and panties with quick, impatient movements, and before Nikki could feel exposed and self-conscious, he'd yanked off his boots, stripped off his jeans, shorts and shirt, and joined her.

His heated weight blanketed her, his mouth and hands quickly driving her delirious with passion.

The clatter of metal meeting a tiled floor was loud in the quiet room, startling Nikki from her reverie. Voices sounded from the hallway outside, followed by muted laughter as hospital staff dealt with whatever had fallen.

Nikki sighed, her mood solemn as she once again

gazed at the remote moon and admitted to herself the painful truth.

She didn't regret giving her virginity to Cully. He was everything her dreams had hoped her first lover would be, and more.

She bitterly regretted the morning after. And she didn't think she could ever forgive him, or herself, for loving him so deeply while she had been nothing more than a one-night stand for him. A fact he'd proved irrefutably when he married Marguerite Sommers a short week later. When Marguerite gave birth to their son five months after that, and Nikki realized that Cully must have been involved with the other woman at the same time he'd been spending the long summer days with her, the sense of betrayal cut her to the bone.

Now she had to try to reach past the pain and bitterness and find a way to deal with Cully Bowdrie for Angelica's sake. The child was too ill at the moment to pick up on the tension between Cully and her big sister, but she was a very bright little girl. As soon as she started feeling more herself, Angelica would notice that all wasn't sweetness and light between them, and she'd ask questions. Worse yet, she'd worry.

Nikki sighed. She'd have to try harder to be pleasant, but just being in the same room with Cully scraped her nerves raw and opened old wounds.

She threw back the afghan and checked on Angelica, brushing a kiss against her forehead. Her heart hurt, love twisting its ties tighter.

No choices left for me, sweetheart. Nikki ignored

the tears that misted her vision. *You're already ex-hibiting all the signs of adoring Cully. I recognize the symptoms. So I'll have to find a way to let him into our lives without a war raging between us. Because unlike his feelings for me, I think Cully loves you right back.*

Nikki stood by Angelica's bedside for a long time, watching her sleep, aching with the fierce need to fight the disease herself and knowing there was nothing she could do but watch and pray.

Finally, she returned to the cot, settled the warm afghan over her once again, and at long last, gave in to exhaustion.

The next morning, Angelica developed a fever, and Nikki's resolve to work harder at being polite to Cully fell by the wayside. All three adults, Nikki, Cully and Cora, spent long hours at Angelica's bed-side, reading to the fractious child when she was awake, tempting her with cold drinks when her ap-petite was nonexistent, and bathing her hot, dry skin when the fever inevitably rose. They spelled off Nurse Phillips, working around the clock to make sure the little girl was comfortable.

Nikki was terrified that Angelica would have a setback that would endanger her life. She couldn't bring herself to leave her side for a moment, barely taking time to hurry downstairs to the cafeteria for a meal, and refusing to leave the hospital to sleep. She lost track of the passage of days and nights, and rejected her aunt's repeated requests that she get more rest.

At last, Angelica went a whole day without an

elevated temperature. The adults around her drew deep sighs of relief.

Nikki glanced at the window and realized that the sun was lowering in the west. She wondered briefly what day of the week it was.

Angelica was sleeping, and Nikki gently tested for fever by touching the child's cheek with the back of her fingers.

No fever. Thank God, she thought, and settled back into the chair, weariness pulling at her. Her aunt's worn hand closed gently over her shoulder, and Nikki looked up at her, infinitely grateful for her comforting presence.

"Nikki," Cora whispered. "I want to talk to you but I don't want to wake Angelica." She nodded toward the door across the room, where Cully stood, hands tucked into his pockets, watching them.

Nikki glanced at her little sister's pale face; Angelica's eyes were closed, her rosebud lips slightly parted in sleep.

Quietly, Nikki eased out of the chair and followed her aunt across the room.

"What is it?" she asked, her gaze moving from her aunt's determined features to Cully's hard stare. "Is something wrong?"

"Not yet," Cully commented. "But there will be if you don't take a break."

"He's right." Cora's decisive nod confirmed her agreement. "You need to get away from this room, Nikki."

"All right," she conceded reluctantly. "I'll go down to the cafeteria for dinner."

"No. I'll take you out to dinner."

"It's very kind of you to offer, Cully, but I'll just run down to the cafeteria and grab a sandwich or something."

"That won't cut it, Nikki." He knew by the way she tilted her chin at him and frowned that she was going to argue. "You need to get away from the hospital for a while."

"Why?"

"Because you're pale and exhausted," Cora said. "You need to rest."

"You haven't been outside the hospital since the bone marrow transplant," Cully stated, his brusque words reflecting impatience.

"That's not true," Nikki protested.

"No?" He lifted an eyebrow. "You've been here every day and you've insisted on staying in the room with Angelica every night. So when, exactly, did you go outside?"

"Well, I..." Nikki frowned. She couldn't remember. She looked at Cora for confirmation. "Surely it hasn't been that long, has it?"

Her aunt nodded, her blue eyes sharp with concern. "Yes, it has. Even the nurses have noticed and commented that you're not taking enough time away from the hospital. And Cully tells me that the two of you have talked about this before. I know you're worried about Angelica, dear, but it won't help her if you let yourself get run-down."

Nikki opened her mouth to protest, but closed it

again without speaking. For the first time in days, she focused solely on her aunt. Cora looked every one of her sixty-plus years, her face lined with worry. Nikki wanted to refuse to go anywhere alone with Cully, but she was unwilling to worry Cora further. "All right. I'll go out to dinner." She glanced briefly at Cully. "Let me comb my hair and put on some lipstick, then I'll be ready."

"All right."

She disappeared into the bathroom.

Cora heaved an audible sigh of relief. "Well." She looked at Cully. "That was easier than I thought it would be. She must be more tired than I figured."

"She's worn-out," Cully growled, frustrated. 'She's so tired that she's practically swaying on her feet. I don't know how she's managed to stay vertical this long."

"I don't, either. She just wouldn't listen when I tried to convince her that she should go back to the hotel and get some sleep while I stayed here with Angelica. That girl can be as stubborn as a mule." Cora stepped closer, lowering her voice. "After you feed her, take her back to the hotel and make her go to bed."

"She won't do it." Cully shook his head. "I'm surprised that she agreed to leave Angelica long enough to go to dinner. I figured there was a real possibility that I'd have to sling her over my shoulder and carry her out, kicking and screaming."

"But you would have done it, right?"

"Damned straight," Cully shot back. "Look at

her. You can almost see her getting thinner every day.''

"Right. That's why I want you to take her to the hotel and make sure she gets some rest, no matter what you have to do to convince her. But you'll have to stay with her. When she's really tired, she walks in her sleep and it's not safe to leave her alone.''

Cully stared at Nikki's aunt. *Stay with her?* Having Nikki alone in a hotel room was a fantasy that figured prominently in his dreams, but none of those fantasies had him guarding her while she slept. He couldn't tell Cora that he doubted he could keep his hands off her niece's too-tempting body if he had to spend the night alone with her. So what alternative did he have? He couldn't think of a single one.

"All right." He agreed, finally, because he knew there was no way in hell that Nikki would let him near her. She hated his guts. "What do I do if she sleepwalks?''

"Try not to wake her. Just speak calmly and quietly to her and guide her back to bed.''

Cully nodded, hoping his face didn't give away the instant image of taking a nightgown-clad Nikki to bed.

The door to the bathroom opened and Nikki walked out. "I'm ready.''

The restaurant Cully drove them to was Italian. The moment he opened the door and ushered her over the threshold, mouthwatering aromas assaulted her with every breath she drew, and Nikki was suddenly ravenous.

"How did you find this place?" she asked after they were seated and given menus. She was determined to maintain a polite reserve.

"The bellhop at the hotel recommended it." Cully flipped open his menu. "I can vouch for the fettuccini alfredo and the lasagna. The ravioli isn't bad, either."

"I think I'll try the fettuccini. Have you eaten here often?" She laid aside her menu with precision, avoiding meeting his gaze by studying the other diners, determined to keep the conversation focused on impersonal subjects and survive the meal without an argument.

"Often enough. I can take only so much cafeteria food before I burn out. I'm surprised you've lasted this long. Didn't the chef in you object?"

She shrugged. "To be honest, I didn't notice. I couldn't even tell you what I've eaten for the last few weeks. I just ordered the cafeteria's special of the day, chewed and swallowed."

"No kidding?" He shook his head in amazement. "Can this be the same woman who told me that I had no taste buds when I told her that all I ever ordered at the Grill was a steak, rare, or a hamburger, burned?"

Her defenses lowered by weariness and the cozy atmosphere of the café, Nikki was caught off guard by the unexpected charm of his slow, teasing drawl. She smiled, despite her determination to be coolly distant and polite. "Let's just say that I'm too tired to lecture you. And you've done a lot to improve your image by bringing me to an Italian restaurant instead of a steak house.''

''Ah. If I'd known that was all it took, I'd have brought you here sooner.''

The waiter arrived, interrupting their conversation. Nikki glanced idly around the restaurant while Cully gave him their orders. They sat in one of a dozen booths lining the walls. Round tables draped in red-and-white-checked tablecloths crowded the floor space and were fully occupied, the room humming with the low buzz of conversation, the clatter of china, the click of silverware, and background music that held the rich resonance of Italy.

''This looks like a family-owned restaurant,'' she commented, making idle conversation to fill the silence that fell when the waiter left their table.

''I think it is.'' Cully glanced around the room. ''See the young girl waiting tables on your left?''

Nikki glanced over her shoulder, her gaze finding a slim teenager. The girl's thick braid of ebony hair brushed against her white T-shirt as she expertly shifted laden plates from her arms to the table.

''Yes. What about her?''

''Her mother is the woman behind the cash register and her father is in the kitchen.'' Cully gestured at another woman wiping crumbs from a tabletop in a vacated booth across the room. ''I'm not sure but I think she's connected to the family.''

''And our waiter?'' Nikki asked.

''I believe he told me that he's a nephew.''

''Interesting,'' Nikki commented, her gaze taking

in the spotless floors, the neatly dressed employees, the smiles on the faces of the patrons filling the tables.

"Does it remind you of the restaurant where you worked?" Cully asked, curious about her life in Seattle.

"No. Not at all. I didn't work in a restaurant that's open to the public. I worked in a senior citizens' assisted living complex."

"No kidding. I thought you were a chef?"

"I was. Actually, I was sort of a combination chef and nutrition expert," she told him. "It was a great job. I especially liked the contact with the residents, who dropped by the kitchen to chat and share a cup of tea with me."

The waiter returned with their dinner salads and a bottle of wine. Cully waited until their glasses were full and the waiter disappeared once more before he said, "I thought you were a chef in an upscale city restaurant."

"I was, for a while, after I finished school." She sipped her wine and glanced up to find him watching her, his long legs stretched out beneath their table and his shoulders relaxed. "This is my favorite wine."

"I know."

"You know?" Surprised, she stared at him. His eyes were unreadable; his fingers turned his wineglass in slow circles on the table. "How did you know?"

He shrugged. "I remembered that you ordered it at The Crossroads one night and said you liked it."

Taken aback, she tried to decipher his enigmatic expression. "I ordered wine one time and you remembered what kind it was?"

"I remember a lot of things about you."

His fingers didn't stop playing with his glass; he still lounged at ease. But the air between them suddenly crackled with tension.

Nikki swallowed, throat dry, unable to look away. Her heart beat faster; her lungs constricted in her chest. Time stretched until it felt like forever, but must have been only moments before his gaze released hers. He glanced at the salad plate on the table in front of her and nodded at it before meeting her gaze once again.

"Try the salad."

Wordlessly, she focused on the greens, grateful when she felt his attention leave her as he picked up his own fork.

"So what happened after chef's school that made you decide to leave the fancy restaurant and take a job in an old folks home?" His tone was even, reflecting not a trace of the heat she'd seen in his eyes.

The thread of sexual tension that had spun between them eased appreciably by his return to their earlier conversation.

"The Eastmont isn't an old folks home!"

"Isn't it? I thought you said it was a place for senior citizens."

"It is, but if you could see the people that live there, I don't think you'd call them 'old folks.' Lots of them jog, swim, travel the world—they're more active than I am, and most of them are forty to fifty years older than me.''

"No kidding? Good for them.''

"That's what I say. Actually, a lot of them remind me of Aunt Cora, only with more money.''

"Because they don't sit around in rocking chairs?''

"Partly. And partly because they have such a deep interest in life and they're so involved.''

"Cora's involved, all right,'' Cully said dryly. "And nobody would dare call her 'old folks'—at least not where she could hear them.''

"True.''

The waiter arrived with their dinner, and for long moments, conversation all but ceased as they ate.

"This is delicious,'' Nikki said after the edge was gone from her hunger. She sipped her wine and searched for a new topic of conversation. "Cora tells me that you bought the old Carmody ranch and that you're living out there.''

"Bowdrie Brothers bought the ranch,'' Cully corrected her. "But yes, I'm living there now. Have been for the last couple of years.''

"I don't think I've ever been out there. What's it like?''

"The land is great.''

"And the buildings?''

"Not as good as the land. I rebuilt the barn and some of the outbuildings, so they're in good shape, but I haven't done anything to the house yet. The building's old, probably built in the mid-forties, but it's structurally solid and keeps the rain and snow out.'' He shrugged dismissively. ''It's a place to sleep and eat, and that's all I need.''

''That's a man's comment if I ever heard one,'' Nikki said, a quick mental image of her cozy apartment flashing through her mind. ''No woman would ever settle for that.''

''Probably not. But then, I don't spend a lot of time in the house, unlike most women.''

''I thought you said that you ate and slept there. That's got to be, what—eight hours of each day?''

''Sure, when I'm home. But I'm away a lot.''

''Really?'' Curious, Nikki couldn't refrain from asking the question that had plagued her in the months since her aunt Cora had relayed the rumors that Cully occasionally disappeared from Colson for weeks on end. ''Where do you go?''

Cully gave up any pretense of eating and leaned against the back of the booth's leather-covered seat. ''Sometimes I stay at one of the other ranch headquarters, if I have business there that takes more than a day.''

''Oh.'' Nikki remembered that Cully and Quinn, under the Bowdrie Brothers name, had bought up several surrounding ranches. Cully could probably stay at any one of them and rarely spend a night at home, she realized.

''Or sometimes I spend a couple of days with Quinn and Victoria.''

''Oh.''

''And sometimes I'm out of town for a while on business.''

''Do you still do most of the buying and selling

of livestock for you and your brother?'' Nikki asked.

"Yeah. I still do,'' Cully conceded. "But in the last few years, I've been out of town fairly often on personal business.''

Startled at the voluntary revelation from the usually reticent Cully, Nikki's eyes widened.

His mouth twisted. "Don't tell me you haven't heard the gossip, Nikki. I'm sure my stepmother has half the population of Colson convinced that I'm off somewhere doing time in prison, or smuggling drugs, or God knows what else her fertile imagination can come up with.''

Startled at his dry comment, Nikki eyed him. "No, I have to admit, I haven't heard any of those.''

"No?'' He leaned forward, pushed back his plate and folded his arms on the tabletop. "So, what have you heard?''

"Most of the stories have you indulging in wild orgies.'' She didn't bat an eyelash as she repeated the whispered, scandalized comment she'd heard from a local white-haired gossip the last time she'd been in Colson.

It was Cully's turn to look startled. "Orgies? No kidding?''

"No kidding. Mrs. Henderson was as serious as a heart attack. Swore she had it from a 'reliable source,' whatever that means.''

"I'll be darned.'' A slow smile curved his mouth. "And from Mrs. Henderson. I never would have thought she could have managed to get the word

orgy out of her mouth without choking and fainting
dead away.''

"She looked a little green when she whispered
it in my ear,'' Nikki confirmed. "So,'' she said as
casually as she could manage. "Where *do* you go
when you leave town?''

"Hunting.''

Nikki blinked. "Hunting? You mean like deer
and rabbits?''

"No. Like people.''

"Like people,'' she repeated slowly, before shaking her head. "I don't understand.''

"I thought Victoria might have said something
to you.''

"About your hunting for people? No.''

"No?'' Cully watched her intently. "How much
do you know about the Bowdrie family history,
Nikki?''

"What do you mean?''

"I mean what gossip have you heard about me
and my brother,'' he said impatiently. "And our
father and mother.''

"Probably only what everyone in Colson has
heard,'' Nikki responded, reluctant to repeat gossip.

"So? Give me specifics,'' he said brusquely.

He demanded a blunt answer. Nikki gave him
one. "The story I heard was that your father was
married to Eileen and that she couldn't, or
wouldn't, have children. He then met your mother
and fathered two children, you and Quinn. Then
your mother left town, leaving you with your father

and Eileen, and your mother hasn't been heard from since.''

Cully's mouth curved in a small smile that didn't reach his eyes. ''Sounds like you've got the bare bones of the story right. What nobody in Colson knows is that Dad searched for our mother until the day he died. In fact, he left a trust that kept detectives searching even after he was gone. Four years ago, the agency contacted us, and we discovered that she was pregnant when she left town.''

Nikki dropped all pretense of detachment and tensed, leaning forward. ''She was pregnant?''

Cully nodded. ''Yes. Pregnant. Seven months later, she gave birth to a baby girl. Somewhere in the world, I have another sister.''

Nikki could only stare at him.

''Is that what you meant when you said that you're hunting people? You're searching for your sister?''

He nodded. ''Yes. We traced our mother to Los Angeles and learned that she accepted employment with a family in the diplomatic service. She and the baby left the country with them when they were assigned to the embassy in Belize.''

''Is Belize one of the places you went 'hunting' for your mother and sister?''

''Not for my mother,'' he corrected, his voice abruptly harsh. ''For my sister. And yes, that's why I was there.''

''Did you find her?''

''No.'' His gaze left Nikki's, a small frown etching lines between his dark brows. ''No, I didn't find her." He looked back at her. "But I need to. Now, more than ever. If Angelica's body rejects my bone marrow, then we need to know how to contact my sister. Maybe she'll be a better match."

Nikki's hand clenched atop the snowy white tablecloth. "She won't reject your bone marrow. She's had a little setback, but the doctor says this is perfectly normal. She's going to get well."

Cully's callused hand closed over Nikki's. Beneath his palm, her hand tightened into a fist. He uncurled it and threaded his fingers through hers. The intimate interlacing of his work-roughened hand with hers made her catch her breath, and tears burned her eyes.

Cully didn't look at her, his gaze fastened intently on their hands, her fingers slender and pale between his darker, blunt-tipped ones. His thumb smoothed small circles over the back of her hand.

"Maybe she's doing okay at the moment, but there's always a chance. And with my track record, it's damned unlikely that I can save her."

Shocked, Nikki stared at him, the mixed emotions raging through her body momentarily forgotten. "What do you mean? Do you know something I don't? Did the doctors say anything to make you think that she'll reject your bone marrow?"

"No."

His gaze flashed up to meet hers. Nikki caught her breath at the deep well of pain in his eyes.

"No," he repeated, his voice gentling to a soothing rumble. "They haven't said anything. I like to hedge my bets, that's all. It couldn't hurt to have a backup plan, could it?''

"No," Nikki agreed. Her voice shook.

He gripped her hand tightly, then released it, sitting back. "Finish your dinner. I promised Cora that I'd be sure you ate more than two or three bites."

Nikki resumed eating and struggled to find a way to broach the subject of Angelica and Cully's father. "Cully, there's something I've been wanting to discuss with you," she finally said.

"Yeah?" His gaze narrowed. "What is it?"

"It's about Angelica." Nikki's fingers twisted her napkin in her lap. "I've been thinking about what you said. I think it's time we tell her that Charlie is her father as well as yours."

Emotion flared in Cully's eyes, then was carefully banked as he stared at her for a long, silent moment. "It's about damn time." His words were blunt, harsh with repressed emotion. "What made you finally decide we should tell her?"

Nikki wouldn't allow herself to avoid his gaze. "We'll have to tell her sooner or later. And I think she needs to know the truth before we all go home. I'm sure the gossip mill in Colson is having a field day with the fact that you're staying here in Denver with us. Once we're back in Colson, anyone seeing you with Angelica will put two and two together and guess that you're related."

"You think there's a family resemblance?"

"Yes. She has the same black hair and the same

coloring except for her eyes. I can see a definite family resemblance between her, you and Quinn."

Cully's gaze narrowed. "And you don't like it, do you?"

The tension that stretched between them was palpable.

"Only because that family resemblance will give the gossips one more thing to speculate about. I freely admit that I'm not looking forward to children teasing Angelica about being the illegitimate daughter of the infamous Charlie Bowdrie."

"I can't say I blame you." Cully's words were clipped. "I've lived with it all my life. I wish I could spare Angelica the notoriety that goes along with being one of Charlie's kids. But I figure it's better if we tell her ourselves, because sooner or later, one of the kids in school will overhear his or her parents talking about the latest Bowdrie scandal and tell her what they heard."

"I know." Nikki sighed. "It won't be easy for her." She steeled herself to be honest with him, refusing to let her own experience with Cully shade her words. "She's grown very fond of you, Cully. She trusts you."

Unlike me. I don't trust you at all. She didn't say the words aloud, but the narrowing of his eyes and the slight twist of his mouth told her that he caught the unspoken message.

He lifted his glass. "Here's to trust."

Nikki lifted her glass in acknowledgment, managing to swallow a small sip of wine, but her appetite was gone. It wasn't long before they left the restaurant and were in the truck, driving back toward the hospital.

Absorbed in her thoughts, Nikki didn't notice that Cully didn't turn left on the street that would take them to the facility. It wasn't until he pulled into a parking space and turned off the engine that she realized where they were.

"What are we doing here?" She tipped her head back to look out the window at the facade of the hotel.

"Cora wanted you to collect some things from the hotel room for her," Cully lied without a twinge of conscience. "She said you should call her from the room and she'll give you a list."

"She didn't tell you what she wanted?"

"No."

"I see." Nikki didn't want to be alone in her hotel room with him. The very thought made her stomach jump with nerves. She glanced sideways at him. "This should only take a few moments. I won't be long."

He ignored her none too subtle attempt to have him wait in the truck, and shoved open his door. "I'll go up with you."

Nikki was intensely aware of him as he held the hotel door open for her and walked beside her across the lobby. A small group of guests waited at the bank of elevators, and their chattering filled the silence. The doors slid open and she found herself carried along as the group surged into the elevator. Cully's hand rested lightly at the small of her back, the connection keeping them together as they stepped to the rear of the elevator. He didn't remove his hand from her waist, and his arm was a warm, hard bar across her back.

She focused on the silver hair of the woman standing in front of her. Despite her effort to hold herself apart from him, the few inches that separated her from Cully were heated by their bodies and made a mockery of her refusal to give in to desire and sink against him. Every breath she drew pulled in the scent of his aftershave, and she felt surrounded by him.

"Hold the elevator!"

Nikki was so distracted by her struggle to deal with her reaction to Cully that the loud plea barely managed to yank her back to an awareness of the other people sharing the elevator. A heavy-set man carrying a suitcase hurried toward the elevator as one of the occupants pushed the button to hold the door open.

"Thank you," he said to the group as he entered, jockeying his luggage to squeeze aboard.

The people crowded together to make room for the newcomer. Those in front stepped back as the doors slid shut, forcing Nikki to step back also, and she was brought up solidly against Cully.

"Sorry," she murmured, and attempted to ease away.

He responded by slipping his arms around her and holding her lightly in front of him. His hands rested on her waist, his fingers splayed against her midriff. One thumb rested just below her breast, and Nikki felt the imprint of each of his fingertips against her skin as if the light cotton of her blouse wasn't there. She caught her breath, her heart hammering. He froze for an instant before his grip tightened and he eased her closer, his chest and thighs branding her back, buttocks and thighs.

Nikki struggled to control her response. All her instincts were at war. She wanted to rest her palms on his thighs and turn her head to find his mouth with hers. She wanted to tear herself from his arms and flee. The press of the crowd that surrounded them prevented her from doing either.

The ping of the elevator broke her absorption with the feel of his heated, hard body against her back. She breathed a sigh of relief when the doors opened on her floor and fully half of the occupants left the car. She moved with them, breaking the contact with Cully, and hurried down the hall.

"What did I do with that key," she murmured. Shaken by those brief moments in the elevator, she refused to look at Cully, focusing instead on the contents of her purse. "Ah, here it is." Relieved, she halted in front of a door and slipped the key card into the slot. The light blinked green and she pushed the door open, stepping inside.

Without commenting, Cully entered behind her, closing the door and shutting the two of them into the room together.

Chapter Six

"Please, make yourself comfortable." She crossed to the telephone on the desk near the window. "I'll phone Cora."

He didn't answer. As she waited for the phone to connect her, Nikki glanced over her shoulder to find him removing his hat. He ran his fingers through his hair, rumpling the black strands before smoothing them. There was something so masculine and endearingly familiar about the gesture that Nikki's heart caught. She looked away from him and focused on the blank wall beyond the desk.

"Hello?"

"Aunt Cora—it's me."

"Nikki, hello."

"Hi. We're at the hotel. Cully told me that you

wanted me to bring some things to the hospital for you. Do you have a list for me?''

"So you're at the hotel? How was dinner? What did you eat?''

Nikki couldn't help smiling at her aunt's brisk, no-nonsense voice. "I had fettuccini, dinner was very good, and yes, we're at the hotel.''

"Is Cully there?''

Nikki glanced swiftly across the room. Cully leaned against the wall near the entrance, his green gaze fastened watchfully on her.

"Yes, Cully's here. Did you want to talk to him?''

"No. I just wanted to know if he was there. Now,'' she began briskly. "I want you to stay at the hotel tonight, Nikki. You need the rest, and goodness knows, it's my turn to sleep here on the cot beside Angelica.''

"Aunt Cora, I don't think—''

"I know you think you should stay here with Angelica.'' Cora cut her off in midsentence. "But you're too exhausted to think reasonably at the moment, so you'll just have to trust me when I say that a full night's rest in a real bed at the hotel will work wonders. You need to take better care of yourself, for Angelica's sake, as well as your own.''

Nikki sighed. Her aunt was adamant, and in truth, she had to admit that she felt as if she could sleep for a week.

"All right, Aunt Cora,'' she said, capitulating. "I'll stay here tonight.''

"Thank goodness." Cora's sigh of relief carried over the line.

"Was there anything you wanted Cully to bring back to the hospital for you?" Nikki asked.

"Cully? Oh, yes, dear. I need to talk to him, please."

"All right. I'll see you in the morning."

"Right, dear. Good night."

Nikki murmured a last good-night before holding out the receiver to Cully. "Aunt Cora wants to talk to you," she explained when he lifted a brow in inquiry.

He pushed away from the wall and crossed the room to take the receiver from her. Nikki transferred the phone without touching him, wary of the effect his nearness had on her. The combination of too many nights with too little sleep and the two glasses of wine she'd had with dinner had her nearly staggering with weariness. Afraid to curl up on the comfortable cushions of the sofa for fear she'd fall asleep, she perched on the wide overstuffed arm to wait for Cully to finish speaking with Cora.

"Yes, Cora." His deep voice rumbled in the silent room. Half turned away from her, one hand holding the receiver to his ear as he listened, the other propped on his hip, he seemed to shrink the room with his presence.

Nikki shifted uneasily, far too aware that she was alone with him, without the buffers of her little sister and aunt, nor the ever-present medical staff at the hospital.

"I will." He looked up, his gaze finding Nikki. "You'd better tell her."

This time, Cully was the one to hold out the phone. "Your aunt wants to talk to you again."

Nikki pushed away from the comfort of the sofa and moved to take the receiver. "Did you want me to pack something for Cully to bring to the hospital for you?" she asked.

"No, dear. I forgot to tell you that I asked Cully to stay in the hotel room with you."

Nikki's eyes widened, her gaze flying to Cully. His face was impassive. "Aunt Cora, that's not necessary."

"I'm afraid it is, Nikki. What if you walk in your sleep? You know that you're more likely to sleep-walk if you're overtired, and I won't get a minute's rest myself if I know you're alone at the hotel."

Her aunt's voice was adamant, and Nikki's mind raced, trying frantically to think of a solution that would placate the older woman and get Cully out of the suite. But she couldn't think of a single one. Her tired brain refused to respond to her urgent demand.

A wave of tiredness washed over her, and it was suddenly too much effort to argue. "All right, Aunt Cora."

With her gaze fastened on Cully's, Nikki told her aunt good-night once more, slowly returning the receiver to its cradle.

"Aunt Cora tells me that she asked you to stay in the suite tonight."

He nodded, his expression unreadable.

"I don't want you here."

"I know you don't. I'm not too crazy about the plan myself." His gaze grazed the length of her before returning to scan her features. "Fortunately, I figure you're too tired to make a pass at me, so I'm probably safe."

Nikki's eyes widened and she caught her breath in a gasp of outrage. "Why, you…!"

His lips quirked, the corners of his mouth curving upward in a reluctant smile. "Honey, I'm almost as tired as you are. You're safe, believe me."

"Promise?"

Solemnly, he drew an X over his heart with his forefinger. "Cross my heart."

"Well," Nikki said, stifling a yawn, "how can I fail to believe you with an oath like that?" She crossed the room to the hallway that led to the bedrooms and bath. "Aunt Cora wanted me to tell you to use her bedroom tonight," she said over her shoulder. She paused long enough to see that he'd started after her before pushing open the door across the hall from her own. "The maid changed the linens today." She moved away from the door when he reached her, stopping with a hand closed around the doorknob to her room. "I hope you'll be comfortable."

"I'm sure I will." He watched her yawn again, and nodded at the room beyond her. "You'd better get to bed before you fall asleep on your feet."

"Good night."

"Good night."

Cully waited until she entered the room and

pulled the door shut behind her before crossing the threshold into the suite's second bedroom. It was a standard hotel room with a queen-size bed, nightstand with lamp, small bureau and closet along one wall. He dropped his hat on the bureau top, yanked his shirt free of his jeans and ripped open the snaps down the front. The sound of running water reached his ears and he paused, listening, then realized that Nikki must be in the bathroom just down the short hall.

The swift mental image of Nikki naked and wet, water streaming over her in the shower, made him shudder. His heartbeat hammered faster, his body surging to attention. Muttering, he swore savagely and shrugged out of the shirt, throwing it on the floor. He sat on the end of the bed and pulled off his boots, standing to unbutton his jeans, then peel them down his legs. Kicking free of them, he left them in an untidy heap on the floor. Then he yanked back the bedspread and sheets, switched off the lamp and climbed into bed, where he slammed his eyelids closed and concentrated on sleep. Two seconds later, his eyes flew open and he frowned at the dark ceiling.

"Dammit." He had to wear those clothes later that week. He threw back the covers, switched on the lamp and rose to pick up his discarded shirt and jeans. He folded the jeans on the bureau and hung the shirt on a hanger in the closet before he stomped back to bed, snapped off the light and fell into bed, yanking the covers up once more.

But try as he might, determined as he was, it was a long time before he could sleep.

A noise woke him. Instantly alert, he glanced at the clock radio on the bedside table. The hands on the green illuminated dial told him that it was 2:03 a.m. The noise came again, a slight thump, as if someone had walked into something.

Maybe someone had.

Cully threw back the covers and grabbed his jeans, shoving his legs into them. He yanked them up and struggled to button them one-handed as he turned the doorknob and pulled the door open.

The hallway was dark, but moonlight found its way into the living room of the suite through the partially drawn draperies. Nikki's slim shape was silhouetted at the end of the short hall for a brief moment. Then she moved out of sight.

Cully hurried after her, reaching the living room just as she pushed the drapes open wider, flooding the room with cool moonlight. Her hands dropped to her sides and she stood motionless, staring out at the night. Unsure if she was awake or walking in her sleep, Cully approached her with slow caution.

"Nikki?"

She didn't respond to his quiet call. He joined her at the window, scanning her face. Her eyes were open as she stared intently out the window, but there was no reaction to his presence, and she was uncannily still.

"Nikki, honey, are you awake?" he said softly.

Again she didn't so much as blink in reaction. She was wearing what looked like a narrow slip that came to midthigh, edged with a deep border of pale lace over her breasts and at the hem. Narrow ribbon straps drew a dark line over each of her shoulders. The moonlight leached the color from the silk that clung to the curve of breasts and thighs, but it had a pattern of some sort, maybe flowers.

He was reluctant to touch her for fear of scaring her.

I hope Cora's instructions were right, he thought, and stepped nearer, reaching out to slowly curve his hand around her upper arm. She didn't flinch away from him and he drew a relieved breath.

Her skin was cool, almost chilly to the touch. He eased his arm around her shoulders and drew her against him. The soft weight of her tucked under his arm and pressed against his side had him catching his breath in an indrawn hiss. The soft swell of her unbound breast branded his chest.

He clenched his teeth and reminded himself that he had to treat her with calm, quiet authority.

"Come on, honey," he said soothingly, his voice raspy with the effort it took to keep from groaning at the feel of her standing docilely against him, their bodies touching from shoulder to knee. "Let's get you back to bed."

He turned her and urged her gently into motion. Locked together, they walked slowly back across the living room and down the hall into her bedroom. The covers were tossed back, and Cully eased her down onto the bed, his hands cupped over the curve of her shoulder. He couldn't resist stroking her silky skin with his thumbs as he gently eased her onto the pillow and tucked her long, smooth legs beneath the sheet. It took only moments to pull the light blanket over her, but his normally rock-steady hands had a faint tremor and his teeth were clenched by the time he finished.

He brushed her hair from her cheek, smoothing the silky strands across the pillow, his gaze lingering on the shadowy outline of cheek and lips, the arch of feathery brows above her closed eyes.

He wanted to crawl into bed beside her and pull her into his arms so badly that it took a fierce act of will to force himself away from the bed and out of the room.

He pulled the door closed behind him and leaned his forehead against the cool wood for long moments, his breathing harsh, before he unclenched his fingers from the doorknob. He crossed the hall, pulled a blanket and pillow from his bed and returned to the door of Nikki's room. There was no way in hell he was going to crawl into bed with her, and the only other way to be sure he'd wake if she decided to sleepwalk again was to block her exit. It took two seconds to shake out the blanket, drop the pillow and lie down, his body barring the door to her room.

It took a whole lot longer for Cully to fall asleep the second time.

Nikki woke to find a narrow bar of sunlight warming the foot of her bed. Disoriented, she pushed her hair out of her eyes, propped herself up on one elbow and blinked at the shaft of golden light that found its way into the room through a gap in the nearly closed draperies.

Her gaze swung to the digital clock on the bedside table, eyes widening as she realized that it was late morning, far past her usual six o'clock wakeup time.

She tossed the covers back and rose, pulling on her robe before finding her way to the bathroom. It took only a few moments to run a brush through her hair, and after splashing her face with cool water and quickly brushing her teeth, she felt marginally awake. The smell of coffee reached her the moment she pulled open the door to the hall, and she followed the aroma to the kitchenette.

"Good morning."

Nikki halted abruptly. Barefoot, Cully leaned against the cabinet, his shirt hanging unbuttoned outside his faded jeans. Her senses still sluggish from sleep, Nikki could only stare at him. His hair was damp, and the faint scents of shampoo and soap lingered in the kitchenette along with the stronger aroma of brewing coffee.

Nobody should look this good before breakfast. His shirt hung open, revealing his chest, and Nikki's stunned gaze moved over one flat male nipple, darker brown against sleek, golden skin, before traveling lower. His body was honed by hard work, his abdominal muscles clearly defined above the low-slung waistband of his jeans. And below the jeans... Nikki swallowed, her gaze shooting swiftly upward to meet Cully's.

He was watching her, his emerald-green stare fastened intently on hers. She doubted he'd misread the fascination she was sure must be written all over her face.

"Good morning." Her voice was throaty, still husky with sleep. She sifted her fingers through her hair and pushed it back off her forehead. "Have you been awake long?"

"Half hour, maybe."

A faint, husky rasp underlay his carefully neutral words. He wasn't unaffected by the intimacy of the morning, either. Nikki fervently wished she could shrug off his impact on her senses, but since she couldn't, she decided to ignore the effect.

Fortunately for her, the coffeemaker chose that moment to gurgle loudly, announcing the end of the brewing cycle. Cully turned away to pull open the cabinet above the sink and take out two mugs. Silently, he poured coffee and handed one of the steaming cups to Nikki.

"Thanks." She sipped, swallowed, and sighed with appreciation, glancing up to find Cully doing the same. "I thought you told me once that you couldn't cook, including making decent coffee. But this isn't bad."

"Not because of anything I did," he said wryly. "The hotel supplies premeasured coffee packets. All I did was drop it in the basket, pour in water and push the start button."

"Oh."

Nikki couldn't pull her gaze from his. The silence thickened, throbbing between them in time to her pulse.

"Nikki, I—"

The telephone rang, cutting him off. Cully turned away from her and picked up the receiver. She was so disappointed at the interruption that she scarcely heard his words until he turned and held out the phone. She looked at it blankly, then at him.

"It's Cora."

"Oh." Nikki took the receiver. "Aunt Cora?"

"Good morning, Nikki." Her aunt's voice carried clearly over the line. "How are you feeling this morning? Did you sleep well last night?"

"Yes, Aunt Cora. I don't remember anything from the time my head hit the pillow until I woke a few minutes ago."

"Wonderful." Satisfaction permeated Cora's tones. "That's exactly what I hoped would happen. Goodness knows you need the rest."

"I feel much better this morning." As she reassured her aunt, Nikki realized that it was true. Getting away from the hospital for several hours, dining on food that didn't come from the cafeteria, followed by long, uninterrupted hours of sleep, had all worked their magic. She felt stronger than the previous evening, her mind clearer, her emotions a bit less fragile. "Did Angelica have a good night? How's she feeling this morning?"

"She only woke twice, and she settled back to sleep easily each time. We've been reading this morning from the new book about horses that Cully brought her. I swear, we're going to have trouble with this child when we take her home. She says she wants to keep one of Cully's or Quinn's horses in the backyard.''

Nikki laughed. "As long as we get to take her home soon, Aunt Cora, I don't care if she keeps a dozen horses in the backyard!''

"Humph. Easy for you to say. It's not your flowers that will be trampled or eaten.''

Nikki heard Angelica's voice in the background just before Cora chuckled. "What did she say?''

"She said that I should remember that horse manure is good for my roses.''

"Ah. Good point, Aunt Cora.'' Nikki listened with a fond smile as her aunt admonished Angelica to drink her juice. "I'm going to take a quick shower and then head back to the hospital. Do you need anything from your room?''

"No, not that I can think of.''

"All right. And remember, Aunt Cora, tonight is your turn. I insist that you leave the hospital for dinner and a good night's rest.''

Cora laughed. "Ah, now that I've been proved correct, you're going to insist that I have a dose of my own medicine?''

"Exactly.'' Nikki smiled, cheered as always by her aunt's teasing. She glanced up, catching Cully's brooding gaze fixed on her mouth, and her smile disappeared as she caught her breath. His lashes lifted, the heat in his eyes palpable, before he turned and left the room. Distracted, she missed Cora's next comment. "I'm sorry, Aunt Cora, what was that?"

"I said that I just remembered a couple of things that I need, if you wouldn't mind bringing them to the hospital with you today?"

"Of course. Let me find a pencil...."

That emotion-charged moment in the kitchen was lost as Nikki jotted down a list of items Cora wanted. Cully disappeared while Nikki showered and dressed, reappearing in time to drive her to the hospital. But he didn't return to whatever he'd been on the verge of saying before Cora's phone call interrupted him. Nikki desperately wished she knew what he'd been about to say.

Cully decided that Cora's phone call had interrupted him just in time, stopping him from saying and doing something he knew he would have later regretted.

It was better for Nikki that he hadn't given in to the urge to kiss her. He doubted he would have stopped at kissing, not with a bedroom only a few feet away and the silence of the empty apartment surrounding them.

The painful truth was that he was far too interested in Nikki Petersen. He always had been, and watching her deal with her very ill little sister over the last weeks had forced him to see Nikki in a whole new light, intensifying his feelings. Gone was the young woman who'd once hung on his every word. In her place was a wise, mature woman with a deep emotional strength countered by a vulnerability that twisted his heart. He'd come close to 'telling her how much he admired her. In retrospect, he was relieved that Cora's call had interrupted him. He wasn't at all sure that he would have been able to conceal the fact that he still wanted Nikki. And he suspected that the wanting wasn't just lust.

He'd hurt her once. He was determined not to hurt her again, and he had nothing to offer her beyond what he was sure would be mind-blowing sex. She deserved more, and he wasn't a man who had more to give.

The reality of just how sterile his life had been for the last four years without her—and how bleak the future seemed without Nikki to share his life— was painful.

Cora was doubtful about the decision to tell Angelica that her father was Charlie Bowdrie, and that Cully and Quinn were her brothers.

"Are you sure this is the right time?" Cora's worried frown searched both Nikki's and Cully's faces. "I'm not saying that she shouldn't be told, but I'm concerned about how she'll take the news. Not that I think she won't be excited to find out that she has two new brothers, Cully," she added hastily. "It's just that she's had so many shocks lately."

"Those were my concerns exactly, Aunt Cora," Nikki told her. "But Angelica has spent a lot of time with Cully over the last few weeks and grown very attached to him. I think the odds are that she'll be excited and happy. And the more time she has before we go home to Colson to get used to the idea that her father was Charlie Bowdrie, the better. There's bound to be a lot of talk around town about her connection to Cully and Quinn, and Angelica's sure to hear it sooner or later. The more comfortable she is with the news, the less the gossip will bother her. I hope.''

''Do you agree, Cully?'' Cora asked.

''Yes.''

Cully's unequivocal response appeared to reassure Cora. The frown smoothed from her forehead. ''All right.'' She squared her shoulders and gestured at the closed door to Angelica's room. ''I'll let you two do the explaining. And I think we should send Nurse Phillips to the cafeteria for a coffee break.''

Cully pushed open the door and ushered the two women into the room ahead of him.

Nikki waited until Nurse Phillips left the room before she began. ''Aunt Cora and I—and Cully,'' she added, ''have some exciting news for you, Angelica.''

''What news?'' The little girl's forehead pleated in a worried frown. ''Is it bad?''

''No, not at all. It's very good,'' Nikki assured her, covering the small hand with her own where it lay against the turned-back sheet. Angelica swiftly laced their fingers together and clung tightly.

''Remember all the times you asked Aunt Cora and me about who your daddy was, and we told you that Mama said she wouldn't tell us his name because he'd gone to heaven?''

''Yes. I remember.''

"Well, that's the exciting news we have to share. We've discovered that your daddy was Charlie Bowdrie. And even though he's gone to heaven and you can't meet him, that means that Cully and Quinn are your brothers."

Angelica's eyes rounded, her mouth opening in a silent gasp. Her gaze flew to Cully. He stood with his arms folded across his chest, leaning against the windowsill.

"You're my brother, Cully? Really?"

The amazed delight in her voice was unmistakable. Cully visibly relaxed, flashing her a swift grin. "Yup. Really."

"Oh, wow. This is so cool." Her fingers released Nikki's and she clapped enthusiastically. "What do brothers do? Does this mean I get to ride your horse?"

The three adults exchanged glances that reflected mixed relief and amusement.

"Sure. Just as soon as the doctor says it's okay," Cully answered.

"Maybe you could loan me a horse." Angelica's brown eyes lit with inspiration. "He could stay at my house and I could ride him every day."

"I don't know about that, Angelica," Aunt Cora interjected. "I don't think a horse would be happy in our backyard."

"But you were saying just the other day that fertilizer for the roses is very expensive, and if we had a horse, we'd have our own fertilizer."

"I can't argue with you there, Angelica. We would definitely have fertilizer," Cora said wryly.

Angelica grinned at Cully. "See? That settles it. We need a horse for the roses and for me to play with. Don't we, Nikki?"

"We'll see." Nikki couldn't bring herself to tell Angelica that a horse in their backyard was impossible. Her sister's face glowed with excitement, and her eyes were alight with anticipation. "We'll talk about it when we return to Colson, okay?"

"Okay."

Angelica switched her attention to Cully, quizzing him in depth in an obvious effort to determine exactly what big brothers could be expected to do with little sisters. She was clearly intrigued by this new facet of her life.

Cully spent the noon hour tempting Angelica to eat her lunch while teaching her the finer points of playing five-card stud poker—thus avoiding any opportunities for private conversation with Nikki.

The orderly had just cleared away Angelica's luncheon tray when the hall door swung open and Victoria appeared, followed by Quinn.

"Quinn!" Angelica's face lit up. "Aunt Cora said I can have a horse! We can keep it in our backyard and he can sleep in the garage!"

"I did not!"

"She did?"

Cora's denial and Quinn's surprised query tumbled over each other, eliciting laughter from Nikki and Victoria and a lazy grin from Cully.

"Yes, you did, Aunt Cora," Angelica insisted, feigning a frown at her great-aunt. "We decided that the horse doo-doo would be good for your roses.''

''I'm not sure my roses need that much...stuff.''

''If you keep a horse in your backyard, you're going to have enough 'stuff' for your roses and all the neighbors' gardens on the block,'' Cully said dryly.

''Yes, but they'll all have beautiful roses,'' Victoria stated. ''And it's free. In Seattle, my mom pays big bucks for Zoo-Doo.''

''Zoo-Doo?'' Angelica's eyes lit with curiosity. ''What's Zoo-Doo?''

''It's elephant doo-doo,'' Nikki told her, enjoying the widening of her little sister's eyes. ''Woodland Park scoops it up, dries it, bags it and sells it every year to raise money for the zoo.''

''Wow. Cool.'' Angelica's brown gaze fixed on her great-aunt. ''See, Aunt Cora? You can have really expensive doo-doo for free and your roses will be *so* pretty.''

Aunt Cora met her great-niece's innocent gaze with a stern look. ''I don't care how expensive or inexpensive the manure is, young lady, I am not housing a horse in my backyard to get it.''

''But, Aunt Cora—''

''That means you'll have to come out to the ranch and visit us more often,'' Cully interjected, effectively stopping Angelica's wail and turning her frown into a swift smile.

''Ooh, really?''

''Absolutely.'' Cully flipped her hat brim over her eyes with his forefinger, and she giggled, pushing the hat upward again. The movement revealed soft, baby-fine dark stubble where thick black hair had been. His heart jolted, but the grin on his face never wavered as he winked at her.

Angelica winked back, an ear-to-ear grin displaying white teeth.

Nikki forced her attention away from the affectionate exchange between Cully and her little sister to greet Victoria. "This is such a nice surprise to see you today. I didn't know you were coming to Denver."

Victoria gave her a quick hug. "Quinn needed to talk to Cully, and we both wanted to see how Angelica is doing."

A quick stab of foreboding sliced through Nikki. Her gaze searched Victoria's face, but she could find no evidence of bad news.

Cully looked up at Victoria's comment, quickly scanning his sister-in-law's features before turning to his brother. "You need to see me about something, Quinn?"

"Yeah. Another report from the detective agency came in the mail day before yesterday."

Cully visibly tensed. "And?"

Quinn shrugged. "And there isn't much to report. It looks like they've run into another dead end."

"Dam—darn," Cully muttered.

"What's wrong, Cully?" Angelica leaned forward, her hand closing consolingly over his forearm, the small palm and fingers pale against his tanned skin.

"Nothing, honey," he soothed, covering her hand with his much larger one. He glanced at Quinn and lifted an eyebrow. Quinn shrugged his shoulders in tacit approval, and Cully turned back to Angelica, patting her hand. "You're family now, angel-face, so I guess you have a right to know. Quinn and I have another little sister."

"You do?" Angelica's amazed reaction was quickly replaced by excitement. "Then so do I! Don't I?"

"Yes. You do."

"Wow! This is so cool. Nikki, we have another sister!"

"Well, actually," Quinn said, shooting an apologetic glance at Nikki, "she doesn't."

"She doesn't? Why not? How come I get to have a new sister and Nikki doesn't?"

"Because you, me and Quinn have the same father," Cully explained patiently. "But Nikki doesn't share any parents with Quinn and me, only with you."

Angelica frowned, her lower lip pouting. "I don't care. I think it's mean that I get to have a new sister and Nikki doesn't."

Cully glanced swiftly at Nikki, his expression inscrutable. "Tell you what, kiddo, you can share her with Nikki if you want, okay?"

"Okay." Angelica brightened. "So what's she like? Where is she? Will we get to see her soon?"

"Well, uh…" Cully looked at Quinn, who'd pulled up a chair on the far side of the bed.

"That's a tough question, honey." Quinn's deep

voice was gentle. "See, the problem is, we don't know much about her."

"You don't? Why not?"

"Because we've never seen her."

"That's not possible." Angelica frowned at him in confusion. "How can you not see your sister?"

"Because we grew up in our dad's house and she went away with our mother before she was born."

"But why didn't your dad take you to see her?"

Cully shifted uneasily in his seat, removing his hat and turning it slowly in his hands. "Well, that's kind of a long story."

"I like stories."

Quinn shot Cully a wry grin that elicited a similar smile. "Yeah, I figured you did," Quinn said.

Nikki listened as he tried to explain to the little girl the convoluted tale of their sibling's disappearance and their father's role in it. Victoria joined the trio, perching on the end of Angelica's bed, while Cora sat in the recliner and Nikki found a seat on the deep windowsill.

Watching Cully, Nikki realized that his brief, carefully noncommittal replies hid deep emotions. With sudden insight, she wondered what untold damage being abandoned by his mother had done to the little boy Cully had once been. Her own mother had been more child than mother to Nikki, but at least she'd been present. She hadn't deserted Nikki and disappeared without further contact.

Nikki couldn't help wondering if she'd ever really known Cully, or if she'd fallen in love with his handsome face and easy smile, and never seen beyond the facade to the man inside.

And with a shock, she realized that during the last weeks spent in his company, she'd grown to admire the scarred, complicated man he'd become much more than the man she'd known four years before.

Stunned by the insight, Nikki didn't have time to absorb this new facet of their complicated relationship. She forced her bewildered thoughts into a box and refused to consider them, instead spending the afternoon entertaining Angelica with the others.

Nikki firmly believed that she would have plenty of time later to assess the revelation of her feelings for Cully. Unfortunately, fate had different plans. Cora, Nikki and Cully had worked out a schedule to rotate staying overnight in the hospital room with Angelica. Since tonight happened to be Cully's turn, he offered his empty hotel room to Quinn and Victoria.

About an hour after Victoria and Quinn said good-night and left for the hotel, Nikki tidied the room, collecting Cora's knitting and her own unread paperback novel in preparation for retiring to the hotel for the night. Cora cuddled a tired and fractious Angelica, reading aloud from one of her favorite books in an attempt to soothe her to sleep. Cully prowled restlessly, leaving the room abruptly, only to return fifteen minutes later. He carried a steaming coffee cup, sipping from it only twice before abandoning it on the windowsill.

Nikki watched him from beneath her lashes,

wondering if worry about Quinn's report from the detective agency had caused his caged pacing.

"...and that's the end."

Cora's voice interrupted Nikki's musings, and she turned to find Cora closing the book on her lap.

"And now it's time for Nikki and me to leave, so you can go to sleep."

Angelica's arms wrapped tightly around her great-aunt's neck. "I don't want you to go, Aunt Cora."

Cora patted her cheek. "I'm just going to the hotel, sweetie. Cully will be here with you all night."

"But I want you to stay." Angelica's little mouth curved downward, her eyes pleading.

"I know you do, Angelica, but it's Cully's turn to stay with you tonight. You wouldn't want to make him think that you don't want him to stay, would you? And hurt his feelings?"

"Nooo." Angelica buried her face against Cora's throat, peering over her shoulder at Cully. "But I want you to stay with me tonight."

Cora's gaze moved to Cully and then Nikki, her eyes reflecting the fact that she was torn.

"Please, can Aunt Cora stay with me tonight, Cully?"

Cully had no resistance to her plea, accompanied as it was by the threat of tears and the distinct trembling of rosebud lips. She was clearly exhausted and he felt a twinge of guilt at the possibility that her excitement at learning that he and Quinn were her brothers and Charlie her real father may have overtaxed her fragile health.

"Sure she can, honey." His deep voice was gentle, all evidence of restless impatience gone as he bent to brush a kiss against her forehead. "As long as that's okay with Cora?" He shifted to look at the older woman.

"It's perfectly okay with me, Cully."

Cully smiled and tapped Angelica's small chin with his forefinger. "There you go, honey. She'll stay. So no more tears, okay?"

"Okay." Angelica managed a watery smile before snuggling closer in Cora's arms, her eyelids heavy with exhaustion. "I didn't hurt your feelings, did I, Cully?"

"No, angel-face, you didn't hurt my feelings."

"Good." Her head nodded sleepily as Cora gently unclasped the little girl's thin arms from around her neck and eased the small body back against the pillows.

Cora straightened, and Angelica's eyes flew open in alarm. "Aunt Cora. You're not leaving, are you?"

"No, sweetheart," the woman soothed, smoothing the sheet beneath Angelica's chin. "I'm just tucking you in so you can go to sleep. I'll be right over there on the cot, where I always am."

"Promise?"

"I promise."

"Okay."

The small fingers loosened their fierce grasp on Cora's and offered no resistance when her aunt tucked them beneath the sheet. Black lashes drifted lower, fluttering briefly before her eyes closed completely. Cora waited a few moments before moving quietly away from the bed to join Cully, beckoning Nikki to join them.

"I'm sorry, Cully," she murmured. "She's exhausted tonight."

Cully waved his hand dismissingly. "No problem. It's pretty obvious that she's worn-out and a little cranky." He frowned, his gaze narrowing on Cora's features before flicking to Nikki. "This doesn't mean she's getting weaker, does it? Should we call the nurse?"

"No." Nikki shook her head. "Even when she's in the best of health, Angelica gets irritable when she's tired. She's always needed at least eight hours of sleep, and she does better with ten. So unless she's running a higher temperature or has some other sign that there's a medical problem, I'm guessing that this is our typical overtired Angelica."

"She doesn't have an elevated temperature," Cora stated. "I'm sure she's just tired tonight. It's been an exciting but exhausting day for her. It isn't every day that a girl learns she has new brothers, a sister-in-law and a niece she didn't know about. That's a lot to take in all at once." She glanced over her shoulder. Angelica hadn't moved in the few moments since she'd last checked. "She seems settled in, thank goodness." Cora turned back to Cully and Nikki. "And the two of you might as well go back to the hotel and get some sleep. I know that you gave up your bed to Victoria and Quinn because you thought you wouldn't need it, Cully, so you can use my room again tonight.''

"Thanks, Cora, but I don't think—" Cully began, hearing Nikki's gasp at her great-aunt's words, but Cora interrupted him.

"I insist, Cully. You absolutely must use my room and get a good night's rest. Besides—" she smiled, eyes twinkling "—if you don't go to the hotel, I'll be forced to insist that you sleep in the cot, which leaves me the recliner or a pallet on the floor. And my old bones would be aching for a week."

"You can have the cot! I can't have your achy bones on my conscience."

Cora chuckled, relieved at his teasing tone. "Good. That's settled, then. Now the two of you scoot so I can get some rest."

She made shooing gestures at them. Giving in to the inevitable, Nikki tucked her paperback into her purse and caught Cora close for a quick hug.

"We'll be here early so you can run downstairs for coffee and breakfast," she murmured, receiving a quick nod from her aunt before she moved on silent feet to Angelica's bedside. She bent and brushed a soft kiss against one petal-soft cheek, reassured when her lips found no evidence of the heat of fever.

She turned and bumped into Cully, who was standing silently behind her. His hands closed quickly around her upper arms to steady her while her own hands instinctively flew upward to rest against his chest. Before she could do more than register the solid warmth of his body touching hers, however, he released her and stepped aside.

"Sorry," she whispered, moving quickly away, her nerves trembling in reaction. Moments later, Cully joined her, reaching around her to pull open the door. She glanced over her shoulder, waving a last good-night to Cora before moving ahead of him into the hall. Neither spoke as they walked to the elevators.

Cully pushed the call button and stared at the closed metal doors. "When we get to the hotel, I'll stop at registration and get a room for tonight."

His voice startled Nikki, and she turned her head to stare at him. His profile was etched sharply against the pale wall beyond. She didn't know whether to be relieved or disappointed at his words.

"You don't have to. You're welcome to use Aunt Cora's room."

He didn't look at her, but a muscle flexed along his jawline. "Thanks, but I think it's better if I check into another room."

"All right."

Conversation was all but nonexistent as they drove the few blocks to the hotel. Nikki's nerves were strung tight and she was far too aware that Cully's earlier restlessness was magnified. The tension that always lay between them was stronger than ever. She wasn't happy that Cora had thrown them together. She'd counted on having the night to deal with her earlier revelation that she might, once again, be in danger of falling in love with Cully.

The lobby was nearly empty when they reached the hotel. Nikki stopped outside the gift and sundries shop, touching Cully's sleeve to gain his attention and just as quickly removing her fingertips when he abruptly halted in midstride to look down at her.

"I need to buy some aspirin." She gestured at the shop on her right. "So I'll leave you here. I probably won't see you in the morning because I want to be at the hospital early tomorrow to relieve Cora."

Cully nodded. "Right. Good night."

"Good night." Nikki turned away, not waiting to watch him walk to the registration desk.

She located a tin of aspirin, collected a local newspaper and exited the shop, to find Cully walking across the lobby toward her.

Chapter Seven

"Cully? Aren't you going upstairs?"

"Not tonight."

She frowned at his short, uninformative response. "I don't understand."

"The hotel is full. There's a sales convention in town."

"Oh, no. What are you going to do?"

"Find an all-night diner and then head back to the hospital."

"The hospital? But where will you sleep?"

He shrugged. "The sofas in the waiting room aren't too bad. I can catch a little sleep there."

"Those sofas have got to be at least a foot shorter than you are."

"True. But the waiting room is quieter than this hotel lobby."

"Oh, for goodness sake." Nikki made up her mind with quick decision. "You'll sleep in Aunt Cora's room tonight."

"No."

"Yes, you will." She eyed his stubborn jaw. "I refuse to explain to Aunt Cora why you slept in the hospital waiting room all night when she ordered you to use her room." She'd never told her aunt about the night she'd spent with Cully, nor how he'd broken her heart not forty-eight hours afterward. And she couldn't tell Cora now. Her aunt had grown to rely on Cully, and clearly felt a fondness for him. Nikki couldn't contemplate destroying any measure of comfort Cora felt in the man who'd become a part of their small family. *Despite how I feel about him.*

He was silent for a long moment. "This isn't a good idea, Nikki."

His voice seemed to stroke her, sending shivers of awareness up her spine, warning her that he was right. But the thought of how upset Cora would be if Cully spent the night trying to sleep in the hospital waiting room overcame her misgivings.

"You're right, it's not. But I refuse to tell Aunt Cora that I let you sleep on a too-short sofa when she specifically ordered you to use her empty bed." Nikki caught his forearm and turned him toward the elevators. Instant heat radiated from the contact and she released her grip the moment he moved. "It's been a long week. I'm guessing you're as tired as

I am. We're adults. We should be able to endure each other's limited company for one night.''

Cully shot her a look of disbelief. Nikki chose to ignore it.

I'm not going there, she told herself fiercely, determinedly keeping her gaze fixed on the opening elevator doors. They stepped inside and she pushed the button for her floor, refusing to acknowledge the tension that vibrated between them.

Somehow, Nikki got through the necessary polite conversation as she reminded Cully where towels for the shower and coffee for the coffeemaker were stored, and said good-night. She was so aware of his presence in the bedroom across the hall, however, that she lay awake for a long time, staring at the ceiling while she tried to come to grips with the earlier revelation that she could still be in love with Cully Bowdrie.

After what he'd done, she couldn't accept the possibility that she still cared.

I should hate him, she thought fiercely. *I do hate him.* Despite his care and concern for Angelica and Cora in the past weeks.

She fell asleep just after midnight.

And awoke to the sound of muted groans. Disoriented, she sat up and glanced at the bedside clock. The illuminated dial read 2:00 a.m.

Another groan broke the early morning silence, and Nikki swung her legs out of bed and stood, quickly crossing the room to pull open the door. The sounds were clearly coming from Cully's

room. Her heart hammering, Nikki shoved open the
door to his bedroom.

"Cully?"

The drapes were open and cool moonlight fell
across the bed where he lay. The sheet was twisted
around his hips; the pillow lay crumpled on the
floor against the far wall. His head moved restlessly
against the cotton-covered mattress, a tortured
frown twisting his features.

Nikki was immediately reminded of the night-
mares he'd had in the hospital after he'd donated
bone marrow, and the hours she'd spent at his bedside.

She sat on the edge of the bed and carefully
closed her hand over the curve of his shoulder.
"Cully?" she murmured, shaking him gently. He
didn't seem to hear her, continuing to shift restlessly, his movements tortured and jerky, one hand
closing into a fist as he muttered words that Nikki
couldn't decipher.

She shook him a little harder, her grip a bit
firmer, her voice a decibel louder.

This time he reacted with the speed of a striking
rattlesnake. One hand closed punishingly over her
wrist, yanking it from his shoulder. Before she
could protest, she found herself flat on her back on
the mattress, Cully looming over her.

"Cully?" Wary of the fierce man bent threat-
eningly above her, she wondered if he was awake
or still dreaming.

The hard body pinning her to the mattress tensed,
his grip tightening where his hands pinned hers to

the mattress. "Nikki?" His sleep-roughened voice held a question. His nostrils flared, his eyes narrowing.

Even in the shadowy dimness of the room, Nikki saw recognition chase the warrior's threat from Cully's features. But her pulse thudded even faster when she saw the heat that replaced hostility, the sexual danger that chased away physical peril. She could see it in his eyes, feel it in the heavier press of his body against hers, the swelling of his sex against her thigh. Only the sheet and her thin gown separated their bodies while heat poured from him, feeding the fire that burned in her veins.

Need so strong it hurt urged her to lift herself against him. Unwelcome and unwanted, the surge of desire was followed by a flood of bitter betrayal. They'd shared passion once. And then two nights later he'd told her that he was marrying someone else. Another woman had felt the press of his weight against her, had known the searing pleasure of making love with him.

Nikki couldn't get past the knowledge that he'd betrayed her with another woman. It colored her every thought of him, tinged every conversation with pain.

"What the hell are you doing in here?" With an abruptness that shocked her, Cully lifted away from her and rolled aside.

"I heard you groaning. I thought you were hurt. I came in to check on you, but you must have been dreaming. You were sound asleep."

He stared at her for a long moment, tension

thickening the air about them. Then he scrubbed a hand down his face. "Yeah, I was asleep. And I must have been dreaming." He gestured at her hands. "Did I hurt you?"

"No." Nikki sat up and slid off the bed. "And you're obviously not hurt, either, so I'll leave and let you get back to sleep."

Cully didn't answer, but the heated space between them pulsed with emotion. Nikki didn't draw a deep breath until she closed the door behind her, shutting her away from his gaze.

It took even longer for her to fall asleep the second time.

Nikki was carefully polite the following morning, Cully responding with brusque monosyllables. Sexual tension spun a web between them, and neither seemed able to erase it.

Fortunately for both of them, Angelica provided a timely, wonderfully welcome distraction when her health underwent a remarkable improvement during the following week. Nikki held her breath, praying that the good news would continue. And it did.

Angelica's doctor called the adults together in his office several weeks later to announce the happy news that she was well enough to be transferred home.

They gathered around Angelica's bed to share the good news with her, and she responded with typical little-girl enthusiasm. "Great!" Beaming from ear to ear, she immediately began gathering and stacking the books spread across her blanket. "Let's pack. When do we leave?"

"Whoa," the doctor laughed, his smile matching hers. "You have plenty of time to pack. We have to work out arrangements."

"Arrangements?" Angelica leaned forward, eyes bright as she scanned the smiling faces of her family. "What kind?"

"Like a referral to the doctor who will be doing your follow-up checks at home, and travel plans."

"Okay. Can I go home after lunch?"

The doctor laughed again. "Maybe not that fast, but certainly no longer than a few days."

Angelica's face fell and the doctor tapped a forefinger on the end of her nose. "Cheer up, we'll get you out of here as fast as we can."

"Promise?"

"Promise. I'll get to work on it right away."

"Good. 'Cause I'm ready now."

Angelica was so excited about leaving the hospital that the adults had their hands full keeping her occupied for the next few days while final arrangements were made. Cully simplified transportation by arranging to have a friend fly Angelica, Nikki and Cora back to Colson in a small private plane. Since he'd driven his truck to Denver, however, he couldn't fly home with the Petersens. Nikki felt a twinge of guilt at the relief that flooded her when she learned that they would be traveling separately. Ever since the night when she'd woken him from a nightmare, she felt as if he were a powder keg with a short fuse and she a lighted match.

The small, luxurious plane touched down at Colson's small airport shortly after noon on a hot, sunny day. A gray Mercedes-Benz was parked next to the single-story terminal. Quinn and Victoria leaned against a glossy fender, Victoria shading her eyes with one hand against the sun's hot rays. Their three-year-old daughter, Sarah, was perched on Quinn's arm.

"Look, Nikki! There's Victoria." Angelica's nose was pressed against the window. "And Quinn. And Sarah is with them!" She waved. "Ooh, they see us! Victoria waved at me."

The little girl was nearly climbing out of her seat with excitement.

"Calm down, kiddo."

"Where's Cully?" Angelica pressed her nose against the thick window glass. "I don't see Cully, Nikki."

"Cully is driving from Denver, remember, Angelica? It will take him much longer to drive his truck back to Colson than it did for us to fly home."

"Oh." Her mouth drooped before she brightened once again. "But he'll be here before too long, right? Because he promised he'd take me to his ranch to see the horses."

"No, angel. He won't be too long."

"Good. I wish this plane would hurry up and stop."

"I'm sure the pilot is hurrying as fast as he can," Cora interjected. She leaned closer to peer out the window. "We're taxiing, and in a few minutes we'll stop and then you can unfasten your seat belt, okay?''

"Okay." Angelica twisted in her seat as the plane slowed. "Now? Can I take my seat belt off now?''

"Not until the plane stops completely," Cora said firmly.

By the time the plane was motionless on the tarmac and the door opened, Quinn and Victoria were waiting, Sarah holding her mother's hand and jumping up and down impatiently.

"Welcome home, Angelica."

"Quinn!" Angelica nearly launched herself into Quinn's arms, hugging him fiercely. He laughed, bending so she could wrap one thin arm around Victoria's neck and plant a kiss on her cheek.

"This is Sarah." Victoria swung the toddler up into her arms. "Say hello, Sarah."

The chubby little girl with her father's black hair and green eyes ducked her head shyly. Angelica had no such reservations and patted Sarah's glossy black curls.

"Hi, Sarah. You're my little sister."

Quinn chuckled. "Actually, I think she's your niece."

"I'm an aunt?" Angelica appeared fascinated by the idea. "Like Aunt Cora?"

"Uh, sort of." Quinn looked at Victoria and shrugged, abandoning further explanation of the complicated family connections.

Angelica was too excited to demand a precise definition of her new status as aunt.

Nikki followed Cora off the plane and was hit with a wave of relief that she was home. The summer sun was broiling, the heat bouncing off the pavement in shimmering waves. She drew in a deep breath and was rewarded by the tang of sage in the breeze that lifted her hair and billowed her gauzy skirt before molding it against her thighs.

"It's wonderful to be home again, isn't it?" Nikki glanced up to find her great-aunt smiling with understanding.

"Yes. It is." Her gaze went past Cora to Angelica, still cradled in Quinn's arms. "Although, as badly as I wanted for Angelica to leave the hospital, I'm feeling a little worried about being so far away from there. What if something goes wrong? What if her body starts rejecting the transplant?"

"Then we'll fly her back to Denver. But that's not going to happen," Cora said stoutly. "Now, let's get this child out of the sun and go home. I'm dying to see how my roses are doing." She urged Nikki forward, galvanizing the small group into organizing luggage.

The excitement of traveling and returning home after so many weeks away exhausted Angelica. Shortly after arriving at the big old Victorian house on one of Colson's wide, tree-shaded streets, Nikki tucked her into bed in her own room. Surrounded by her favorite stuffed animals, the little girl shut her heavy eyes and slept peacefully.

Nikki tiptoed out of the room and into the hall, leaving the door ajar, and went back downstairs. The high-ceilinged rooms were cool, the shades on the lace-curtained windows half-drawn to block out the afternoon heat. Ceiling fans turned lazily, stirring the air in the quiet rooms. Nikki followed the murmur of voices to the screened back porch, where Cora, Quinn and Victoria were seated at a white wicker table. A pitcher of lemonade sat at Cora's elbow.

"There you are," Cora greeted her. "Is she sleeping?"

Nikki let the screen door slap shut behind her and dropped into a high-backed wicker chair.

"Yes. She was asleep as soon as her head hit the pillow. All the excitement must have exhausted her."

Cora poured lemonade and handed Nikki a moisture-beaded glass.

"I think she's as glad to be home as I am," Cora commented. She pushed out of the cushioned wicker chair and stood, lemonade glass in hand. "I'm going to make the rounds of my garden and see if Junior watered and fed my roses like he promised."

Nikki smiled. Cora insisted on referring to their next-door neighbor as Junior, even though he was on the shady side of sixty.

"Sarah and I will go with you." Quinn stood, the little girl perched happily on his hip. His boots thudded softly against the painted wood floor as he crossed the porch to hold the screen door for Cora before following her down the steps.

Nikki and Victoria sipped the icy lemonade, their gazes following Quinn's tall figure and Cora's shorter one as they crossed the lawn to inspect the flower garden. Sarah's chatter drifted to them on the warm summer air.

"I can't tell you how wonderful it is to have you all home again," Victoria commented. "Even though we flew to Denver several times and Cully called us from the hospital with updates every week, it's not the same as being able to drive into town and visit."

"It's lovely to be home," Nikki agreed.

"How are things between you and Cully?"

Nikki tensed. "What do you mean?"

Victoria leaned across the table and closed her fingers over Nikki's forearm. "Honey, this is me. Victoria. I'm the one who was falling in love with Quinn when you were falling in love with Cully four years ago. I remember very well how you felt about him and how he broke your heart when he married someone else."

Nikki drew a deep breath. "Yes, well..." She managed a small smile. "We aren't exactly best friends, but we're both trying to remain civil for Angelica's sake."

"That's got to be tough."

"You're right. It is."

Silence reigned as the two women sipped lemonade and gazed out at Cora's sunny backyard.

"That was the oddest thing," Victoria said reflectively.

"What's that?" Nikki glanced across the table. Victoria's eyes were narrowed thoughtfully, a small frown pleating her brow.

"Cully's marriage." Her gaze left the garden and moved to Nikki. "Quinn was the one seeing Marguerite occasionally before I moved to Colson. When Cully showed up at the door one day and told us that he'd married her, Quinn was as surprised as anyone else. And Cully refused to explain."

Nikki was silent. She didn't know what to say, nor if she could respond even if she wanted to. The subject of Cully's marriage to the beautiful divorcee was so painful that she had never discussed it with anyone, not even Cora. And she'd never told anyone, not even Victoria, about the night she'd spent with Cully, nor his announcement forty-eight hours later that he was marrying someone else.

"And the marriage itself made no sense whatsoever. Cully refused to bring her to visit us at the house. I would probably never have met her if I hadn't run into them at the doctor's office one day, and even then he seemed reluctant to introduce us."

"That is odd." Nikki thought it was more than odd. She thought it was downright bizarre. "If she was good enough for him to marry, certainly she was good enough to introduce to his family."

"You would think so, wouldn't you? But I swear the air was so thick I could have cut it with a knife. I got the impression that they didn't even like each other, so why they married is a complete mystery."

Nikki laughed, the sound bitter. "I think we all know why they married. She was pregnant." *And she must have been already pregnant when Cully and I made love, because the baby was born five months later.* The knowledge was a dull blade in her heart, an ache that never quite went away.

"Well, yes, there is that," Victoria agreed reluctantly. "And he must have felt something for her, because every year in August around the anniversary of the car wreck that killed Marguerite and the baby, Cully grows impossible. He becomes moody and difficult, and he isolates himself at the ranch, so we hardly see him for a month or two. Still, I can't get over the feeling that there was something more behind that marriage. It just didn't make sense."

"Yes, well…" Nikki stood. "Lots of marriages don't make sense. We may never understand it." She nodded at the sun-drenched yard. "Let's join Cora and see if she's happy with her roses."

"All right." Victoria accepted the not-so-subtle change of subject and joined her.

Fortunately for Nikki's peace of mind, Cully called shortly after he returned to Colson to tell them that he was swamped with work at his ranch. Because he'd been away in Denver for so long, there was a huge backlog of work that he had to take care of before he could visit Angelica. But he assured her that Quinn had promised to collect Angelica and take her to visit the horses at the Bowdrie Brothers main ranch.

Angelica was disappointed that she wouldn't be seeing Cully immediately, but the promise of a visit with Quinn, Victoria and Sarah at their home brightened her. She returned from the visit later that week beaming with delight.

It was nearly two weeks later before Nikki and Angelica saw Cully, in downtown Colson.

"Mmmm. I love ice cream," Angelica said blissfully.

Nikki tucked her change into the pocket of her shorts and glanced down just in time to see Angelica lick one full circle of the double scoop cone before she bit off the top swirl of chocolate fudge.

"I can see that," Nikki commented dryly. She caught up a handful of napkins, smiled her thanks at the girl behind the counter and pulled open the outer door of Annie's Café. "Come on, kiddo, let's go."

Her attention focused on her ice-cream cone, Angelica walked outside, nearly colliding with a middle-aged couple just entering the café. Nikki caught Angelica's bare arm and steered her adroitly to the left, just managing to avoid an accident.

"Sorry," she murmured.

"No problem." The matron's gaze observed Angelica's concentration on the melting ice cream and exchanged an understanding, amused grin with Nikki.

"Angelica, you've got to watch where you're—" Nikki turned back to her sister, already two steps away down the hot sidewalk.

The warning came too late. Angelica walked into someone. Hands deftly caught her upper arms, preventing her from pitching headfirst against a white cotton shirt.

"Oops. Careful there, angel-face." The deep tones held amusement.

"Cully!"

Angelica threw her arms around his waist and hugged him enthusiastically, the chocolate cone wobbling precariously.

"Angelica!" Nikki grabbed the cone a fraction of a second too late. When Angelica leaned back to grin up at Cully, a dark smear of chocolate smudged the front of his white shirt. "Oh, drat."

Exasperated and distracted, Nikki handed the ice-cream cone back to Angelica and dabbed at the melted ice cream with the handful of paper napkins. Cully sucked in his breath at her touch, the hard muscles of his abdomen flexing beneath her finger-tips.

She yanked her hand away from him. "Sorry."

"No problem." His tone was just as brusque. He looked down at Angelica. "So, how have you been, angel-face?" He tweaked her nose. "You must be spending time in the sun because you're turning brown."

She wrinkled her nose. "I'm outside a lot. Nikki says that I'm rebelling because I had to be inside for so long at the hospital." The last bite of ice cream and crunchy cone disappeared, leaving a smudge of chocolate that quickly disappeared with one swipe of her tongue.

"Makes sense." His unreadable gaze flicked to Nikki, then back to Angelica. "I heard that you liked Quinn's horses."

"Oh, yes, I did." Angelica's face took on a dreamy expression. "They were terrific."

"How would you like to take a run out to my place and look at mine?"

"Oh, yes!" She bounced up and down. "Now? Can we go now?"

"If your sister says it's okay."

Angelica spun and caught Nikki's hand in both of hers. "Please can I go, Nikki? Please?"

Nikki's first instinct was to refuse. She still had difficulty letting Angelica out of her sight, even waking up frequently during the night to check on her. Letting her go home with Quinn and Victoria for the afternoon was one thing, letting her drive off with Cully was another matter entirely.

"I don't know if now is a good time, Angelica. You haven't had your nap and the doctor was very firm about you needing to rest every afternoon."

"We'll only be gone a couple of hours. I'll have her home before dinner." Cully's gaze hardened when Nikki didn't answer immediately. "All right, an hour then. She'll still have time to take a nap before dinner."

"All right," Nikki agreed reluctantly.

"Yippee! Let's go." Angelica tugged on Cully's hand, skipping two steps before stopping. "Where's your truck?"

Cully's deep chuckle earned him an answering grin from the little girl, and Nikki felt her heart twist.

"My truck's across the street."

Angelica tugged him forward two steps and

halted abruptly at the curb to peer over her shoulder. "Come on, Nikki, we only have an hour."

"Oh, no, kiddo. You go ahead. I've got lots of work to do for Aunt Cora this afternoon."

"No, you come with us. I want you to see the horses, too."

One glance at Cully's impassive face was more than enough to convince Nikki that he didn't share Angelica's desire for her company.

"I don't think so, not this time. You go with Cully, Angelica, and maybe I can see the horses the next time you visit them."

"But I want you to come with us now."

A glimpse of pink gingham just beyond Cully distracted Nikki, and she nearly groaned aloud. Hovering in the background, her hand on the doorknob to the café, stood Marian Hollowell. Not only was the middle-aged woman one of the biggest gossips in Colson, she was also a good friend of Eileen Bowdrie, Cully's stepmother. Nikki was well aware that Marian would love nothing more than to overhear an argument between her and Cully over Angelica. The avid expression on Marian's plain face changed Nikki's mind as nothing else could. She'd be damned if she'd do anything to fuel gossip that might hurt Angelica.

"On second thought, a ride out to your ranch to see your horses sounds like a lovely way to spend the afternoon, Cully." She smiled sweetly at him, and though he didn't scowl at her, she didn't miss the swift flash of suspicion in his eyes. She purposely looked past him and smiled at Marian. "Hello there, Marian. Lovely day, isn't it?"

"Yes, indeed it is, Nikki." The woman stared at Angelica. "And this must be your little sister. I'm sure you're pleased to have her out of the hospital and home with you."

"Yes, we are."

"And I hear that you've also taken quite an interest in little Angelica's welfare, Cully. I understand that you even stayed in Denver and visited her at the hospital."

Cully ignored her second comment and answered the first without really telling her anything. "Angelica is an interesting little girl." He cupped Nikki's elbow in his palm and turned her toward the street. "Afternoon, ma'am."

The woman quickly disappeared into the café, where she hurried to join several other women at a table. The group all turned at once to stare out the big plate-glass window at the trio.

"Nosy old bat," Cully muttered under his breath while they waited for two trucks and a sedan to move past on the street.

"I beg your pardon?"

"Nothing."

Angelica tugged on his hand. "I thought you called her an old bag."

Cully met her solemn-eyed stare and shook his head in mock astonishment. "Me? Would I do such a disrespectful thing?"

"I don't know." Angelica leaned closer and

whispered loudly, "Aunt Cora says Mrs. Hollowell is a pain in the keister."

Cully laughed out loud. Nikki swallowed laughter and shook her head at the little girl. "Angelica, that's not something Aunt Cora would want you to repeat."

"I don't see why not. It's true, isn't it?"

Before Nikki could respond, Cully tightened his grip on her elbow and stepped off the curb. Nikki lengthened her stride to keep up with him, while Angelica skipped along beside them.

"It's a little too hot to be running," Nikki muttered.

"What's that?" Cully yanked open the passenger door to his pickup before he released Nikki's elbow, then caught Angelica at the waist and swung her up into the cab. She giggled, her eyes rounding as her feet left the ground.

"Never mind." Nikki stopped him before he could do the same with her. His big frame was too close, invading her space, subtly threatening. "I'm perfectly capable of climbing into a truck."

"And I'm perfectly capable of putting you in," he said evenly.

The words themselves were harmless, but Nikki had no doubt that he was capable of tossing her into his truck if she didn't climb in willingly.

"I'm sure you are," she responded, just as carefully. "Just the same, I prefer to do it myself."

He stared at her for a long moment, a muscle flexing in his jaw. Then he stepped back, easing the tension between them, and gestured toward the open door.

Wordlessly, Nikki turned and stepped toward the cab. Bracketed between the open truck door and Cully's body, she felt a moment of panic when he stepped forward as she swung her legs inside, and her bare knees brushed the soft denim of his jeans. He closed the door behind her and she drew a deep breath of relief.

The drive to Cully's ranch passed relatively quickly. Angelica chattered nonstop, peppering Cully with questions about the truck's interior— everything from the state-of-the-art CD player to the proper use of the cattle inoculation kit lying on the dashboard. She didn't appear to notice that her older sister barely spoke at all.

Cully turned off the highway and onto a well-graded gravel lane that led to a cluster of ranch buildings. Dust billowed up behind the truck. Curious, Nikki scanned the place as they pulled into the yard and Cully parked in front of a big barn. The corrals, barn and other outbuildings were freshly painted and well maintained, but across the wide yard, the house, surrounded by a fence-enclosed, overgrown lawn, was a startling contrast.

Cully pulled open the truck's passenger door, drawing Nikki from her perusal of the house and grounds.

"Hurry, Nikki. I want to see the baby."

Chapter Eight

"The baby?" Nikki slid out of the truck, puffs of dust rising as her sandals reached the ground. "What baby?"

Angelica jumped down beside her. "The new baby horse. She's only two weeks old. Weren't you listening when Cully told us about her?"

Cully threw her an unreadable glance.

Nikki ignored him. "No, I guess I wasn't."

"The mare and foal are in here." Cully gestured to the open doors of the big barn behind him.

Nikki let the two of them lead the way, following more slowly behind.

The interior of the barn was shaded, several degrees cooler than outside and redolent with the scents of hay, saddle leather and animals. Stalls lined the wide aisle, and as they neared the middle of the long barn, a bay mare poked her nose over a stall door and whickered, her ears pricking forward.

Angelica hurried ahead of Cully, stopping abruptly at the stall. The mare didn't startle at the little girl's quick movements. Instead, she peered at her with liquid brown eyes full of curiosity. In the roomy stall behind her, a foal stirred, shifting straw aside as she climbed to her feet.

"Oh, look! It's the baby!" Angelica's voice held awed delight.

Cully and Nikki joined her, one on each side, leaning against the stall gate to watch the baby. The long-legged little foal had the same markings as her mother, with a black brush of a tail and a short, inky mane that fell forward between her ears to fringe her wide eyes. Although her mother was calm, bumping her nose against Cully's arm where it lay on the top of the stall door in a bid for affection, the foal was all jumps and jerky starts as she raced around the space. She jolted to a halt, eyeing the newcomers with misgivings, before she bolted to her mother, nudging against her side.

The mare ignored her and the little one clung to her side, big brown eyes peering out at them through the black fringe of her forelock.

"She's so cute!" Angelica laughed aloud at the foal's antics.

"Yes, she is," Nikki agreed, charmed by the foal.

''What's her name?'' Angelica peered up at Cully.

''She doesn't have one yet.'' He tipped his head and met her gaze. ''How would you like to name her?''

''I'd love to. Really? I can choose a name for her?''

''Sure.'' He glanced at the mare and foal, then back at Angelica. ''As long as it's not something like Daisy or Petunia. I don't want the rest of the guys laughing at me when I register her.''

Angelica eyed him doubtfully.

He winked and pulled gently on her earlobe. ''I'm teasing. You can pick any name you want.''

''Great.'' She giggled and ducked away from his hand.

They watched the baby and mother for several minutes more before Cully stepped back from the gate.

''Most of the horses are farther away from the barn in a pasture north of the house, but I kept three of my favorites in the corral this morning.'' He gestured down the aisle toward the back of the barn. ''This way.''

They left the relative cool of the barn for the heat of bright sunlight. Nikki shaded her eyes against the light and narrowed her eyes to observe the three horses inside the corral.

A dark bay with a black mane and tail, a dappled gray, and a black with a white blaze and one white stocking lifted their heads as Nikki, Cully and Angelica reached the corral rails. They were beautiful, with long legs, glossy coats and an alert intelligence in their dark eyes.

"The black was sired by Jericho, Quinn's stallion." Cully climbed the fence, swinging his long legs over the top rail to sit, his boot heels hooked over the second rail below. Angelica clambered up beside him, copying his movements, wobbling when her flat-soled sandals slipped on the wooden rail.

Nikki, her heart in her throat, held her tongue, but breathed a sigh of relief when Cully casually anchored the little girl with a hand on her waist. Then Nikki followed them, pausing several rungs lower, where she could cross her arms on the top rail and rest her chin on her stacked hands.

"Can I ride them, Cully?" Angelica asked.

"Sure. I'll saddle Gambler, the gray, and you can take a few turns around the corral." Cully nodded at her sandals. "You'll have to wait until we get you some boots to do any serious riding, though."

"Okay."

Cully looked past Angelica and met Nikki's gaze. Tension sizzled between them.

"Think the doc would have any objections to Angel sitting on a horse this afternoon?" His deep voice carried no hint of the tension that heated the space separating them.

Nikki's reply was carefully casual, purposely calm. "No, as long as she doesn't get overly tired."

"Hear that?" He winked at Angelica. "No talking Gambler into bucking or racing."

Angelica giggled. Cully stepped down from the

fence, catching her around the waist and swinging her to the ground beside him.

"I'll wait for you two out here," Nikki said.

"Right." Cully turned and went into the barn, Angelica trailing after him. Moments later, still followed by Angelica, he entered the corral from a door that led into the barn, slipped a rope around the gray's neck and disappeared back into the barn with the horse and little girl.

All around Nikki, the ranch dozed in the afternoon heat. Occasional murmurs and bursts of girlish giggles drifted from the barn's interior. After several years spent in the Pacific Northwest, where summers were cooler, Nikki appreciated the warmth of the sun on her bare legs and arms. She grew sleepy in the quiet heat, stifling a yawn just as Cully walked back into the corral, leading the gray with Angelica perched in the saddle.

"Look, Nikki! I'm riding." She beamed with excitement.

Nikki straightened and waved, laughing back at the crowing little girl. "I see."

Cully patiently led the horse around the corral, pausing often to respond to Angelica's many questions and explain about the saddle, the bridle or the animal.

Far sooner than Angelica wanted, Cully led Gambler across the corral and lifted her out of the saddle, sitting her down next to Nikki.

"That's enough for today. I don't want you getting too hot or tired." He glanced at his watch and then at Nikki. "And we're running out of time. I promised your sister that I'd get you home in time for a nap.''

Despite her protests, he led Gambler away into the barn.

Nikki and Angelica climbed down from the corral fence, waiting until Cully rejoined them.

''I'm thirsty,'' Angelica announced as he neared. ''And hungry. Do you have any lemonade and cookies, Cully?''

''Angelica,'' Nikki chided gently. ''It's not good manners to ask your host for food.''

''But it's perfectly all right to ask family.'' Cully's unreadable gaze flicked over Nikki before he grinned at Angelica. ''I don't have lemonade, but there's soda in the fridge and I bet we could find a box of cookies in the pantry.''

''Great!'' Angelica's face lit with satisfaction. ''Can we go look for them now?''

''Sure.''

Angelica paused for one last glance through the poles at the three horses, then grabbed Cully's hand. ''Let's go.''

Nikki followed more slowly. The big ranch yard was graveled and her sandals kicked up puffs of dust as she walked, the sun hot on her bare head. Ahead of her, Cully's Stetson and Angelica's floppy denim hat shielded their heads from the sun, his long legs covered in faded denim while her sunbrown legs were bare beneath the hem of blue shorts. Every couple of steps, she skipped to catch up with his long strides.

Angelica was quizzing him about the foal, but

Nikki couldn't hear his murmured replies. She was content to let them forge ahead while she followed leisurely behind, glad of Cully's inattention while she satisfied her curiosity about his house.

The neat, freshly painted outbuildings were a stark contrast to the weather-battered house. Traces of faded white paint were still visible on some of the boards, but mostly the house was gray. She tipped her head back, narrowing her eyes against the strong sunlight, and stared at the roof, where patches of new shingles splashed bright color against weathered sections. Despite the lack of care, however, the lines of the old two-story house were solid and strong, with no sag to the roofbeam, no bowing of its square corners.

The only aspect of the house that was clearly new was the unpainted wooden fence and gate that surrounded it. Nikki caught her breath in a silent gasp as she drew near enough to view the lawn. The sturdy fence encircled an expanse of lawn, trees and old garden that was tangled and unkempt. Even if Cully hadn't told her that he had repaired the outbuildings but done little to the house, Nikki would have realized the obvious.

This was a garden and lawn uncared for and unloved.

Nikki was hardly aware that her steps slowed as she passed through the gate, nor that she stopped completely several feet from the porch while she stared curiously at the yard. A huge old maple tree shaded the far corner. Just beyond, a tangle of climbing roses, glowing hot pink, nearly obscured an iron bench, the white paint peeling away to reveal orange rust beneath.

A series of narrow, shallow ditches crisscrossed the yard at intervals, the silvery shine of water obscured in places by clumps of long green grass and overgrown flower beds choked with weeds.

"This is amazing." Hostility forgotten for the moment, Nikki looked at Cully and spread her hands. "This is absolutely amazing. Where does the water come from?"

"From a spring in the grove just behind the house." Cully joined her and scanned the yard, hands on hips.

"I've never seen anything like it," Nikki said, dazed. "It's summertime. Any other garden left untended would have dried up and blown away by now."

"This one would have, too, if it weren't for the water." He pointed at the shallow ditches, most only a few inches deep. "The old guy we bought the place from told me that his wife was from Iowa and she loved gardening. He rigged up a system of little irrigation ditches so she could have a house garden like the one she'd left behind."

A small hand slipped into Nikki's. "It's just like the secret garden in my book, isn't it, Nikki?" Angelica's voice was faintly awed.

"I don't know, kiddo. Do you think so?"

"Yes, I do." Angelica nodded emphatically. "We should make it come alive again." She gazed solemnly at the adults. "We could, you know. We Petersens are gardening women."

Nikki smiled with amusement. Angelica repeated Cora's favorite phrase with just the right emphasis and inflection, sounding so much like her great-aunt that it was uncanny.

"You think so?" she replied.

"I know so." Her silky black curls bobbed as she nodded. "And that would be a nice thing to do for Cully, wouldn't it, Nikki? Because he's going to give me riding lessons, I have to do something nice for him in return."

"Well, I don't know," Nikki said slowly, desperately trying to think of a way to distract Angelica before she committed them to spending hours and hours in Cully's garden. In Cully's company. "I think it would be lovely for you to do something nice for Cully in return for riding lessons, but I'm not sure he wants us in his garden."

"Do you, Cully? Would you like us to make your garden pretty?"

Cully's enigmatic gaze moved from Angelica's excited face to Nikki's wary features.

"Sure," he drawled. "I think it would be great if you fixed my garden." He looked assessingly at the tangled area and shook his head. "But it looks like a job for a bulldozer to me. It's a mess."

"We can fix it," Angelica declared. "Ab-so-lute-ly."

Nikki bit back a groan and resisted the urge to snarl with frustration. *He knows very well that I didn't want to agree to this,* she thought. *And still he encouraged Angelica.*

"Nikki? Nikki?"

Belatedly, Nikki realized that Angelica was talking to her.

"Hmm? What is it?"

"You don't look happy." Angelica's worried, too-sharp gaze swept searchingly from Nikki to Cully and back again. "Are you mad at me and Cully?"

A wave of guilt washed over Nikki. *How could I have forgotten that she's so perceptive?* "No, Angelica, I'm not. I think it's very good of you to want to make the garden healthy again, and I'm sure Cully appreciates your offer."

Even though I don't. Nikki was sure that not a muscle twitched in her face as she looked at Cully. His eyes darkened, telling her that he wasn't fooled by her even words or her calm features. But she looked away from him and met Angelica's worried gaze, relieved to see the concern ease from her face.

Exhausted by the afternoon visit to Cully's ranch, Angelica didn't protest when Nikki suggested that she have her bath and be tucked into bed early that evening. Cora left soon after to attend her weekly bridge club, leaving Nikki the only one awake in the quiet house. She padded barefoot onto the front porch and curled up on the swing, the white-painted board surface cool beneath her bare legs. She dropped her head back, gathering the thick length of her hair in one hand and letting it spill free over the back of the swing. Her nape and throat were blessedly cooler with the heavy weight of hair lifted.

From somewhere down the block, the sounds of muted music and laughter drifted through the dark. The scent of roses in the flower bed edging the porch floated sweet and heavy on the warm night air.

The quiet of the dark street was broken by the purr of an engine. Curious, Nikki shifted against the seat and idly watched as a pickup passed beneath the streetlight at the end of the block. It wasn't until the truck slowed, the headlights arcing across the porch when the pickup turned into her driveway, that she realized it belonged to Cully.

All the quiet ease of the evening vanished, giving way to tense awareness.

The engine died, the headlights shut off, then the driver's door opened and the interior light came on, illuminating Cully briefly before the door closed, immersing him, the truck and the driveway in darkness once again.

The end of the porch where she sat was farthest from the driveway, the chain-hung bench cloaked in shadow. Cully was clearly unaware of her presence as he mounted the shallow steps, crossed the porch and lifted his hand to knock on the screen door.

"If you're looking for Aunt Cora, she isn't home."

Cully's hand froze bare inches from the door frame. He turned his head, his narrowed gaze searching for and finding her in the shadows. "Actually, I was looking for you."

Nikki tensed. "Really? Why?"

He walked toward her, halting beside the swing. He took off his hat and gestured toward the vacant space. "Mind if I sit down?"

Nikki wished he'd chosen to retrieve one of the wicker chairs from the other end of the porch, but refused to suggest he do so. He might take it as a sign that she was afraid to share the swing with him. "No." She pulled her knees closer. "Have a seat."

The swing rocked gently under his weight and Cully leaned forward to drop his Stetson on the porch floor beneath the seat. "Is Angelica asleep?"

Nikki nodded. "She went to bed an hour or so ago."

"Ah." He nodded.

Silence stretched. His jean-clad thigh was mere inches from her toes, the heat from his body reaching across the space to enfold her. He smelled like clean soap and aftershave, scents so familiar that her heart ached in recognition.

She dragged her thoughts away from the fit of faded jeans over powerful thigh muscles, the contrast of his white T-shirt against sun-darkened skin, and thick black hair that tempted her fingers, making them itch with the urge to touch.

"So." She paused to clear her throat, her voice faintly husky. "You wanted to see me?"

"Yeah." He leaned forward, resting his forearms along his thighs, and turned his head to pin her with a fierce green stare. "We have to talk."

Every muscle in Nikki's body clenched with apprehension. "About what?" she asked warily.

"About finding a way to stop sniping at each other," he said bluntly. "Angelica is too smart not to pick up on the tension between us. This afternoon was just the beginning. We've got the rest of our lives to share her, and there's no way she's going to let us avoid each other. As a matter of fact, I get the impression she's hell-bent on keeping us in the same place at the same time."

"I know," Nikki conceded. "And I'm trying not to let my..." She paused, searching for the right word. "Our past relationship affect the present situation."

"Well, it's not working," he said grimly.

She hated to admit he was correct, but she forced herself to be honest. "You're right. It's not."

He looked away from her, staring out at the dark shapes of trees and bushes between porch and street. His profile was a dark outline in the shadowed porch.

"So what are we going to do about it?"

Nikki's sigh was a soft expulsion of sound in the quiet night. "I don't know. I'm trying, Cully, I really am. I don't know what else I can do."

He didn't look at her. "I know you don't want to talk about what happened with us, Nikki," he began. She made an inarticulate sound of protest, but he cut her off. "Please. Let me finish. I've never wanted to talk about it, either. Not with you, not with anyone else." His gaze met hers, his voice husky with emotion. "I didn't lie to you that night we spent together, Nikki. I didn't use you. And it wasn't a one-night stand. It meant more to me than

I can ever tell you. When I wrote the note and left you sleeping at your apartment, I had every intention of coming back that night.''

Nikki was stunned. In any of the confrontations she'd imagined over the years, she'd never once considered that he might have an explanation for his actions beyond out-of-control lust that he later regretted. She scrambled to adjust.

''But…if you meant to come back, why didn't you?''

''Something happened that afternoon, something that involved other people and made it impossible for me to see you again.''

''I don't understand.'' Nikki shook her head, dazed. ''How can that be?'' Then she realized what he meant and confusion gave way to bitterness. ''I see. You mean you learned that Marguerite was pregnant with your baby and you had to marry her.''

''She told me she was pregnant,'' Cully agreed, his voice grim. ''But not with my kid.''

''Not with your…'' Nikki's hands gripped her knees so tightly that her knuckles turned white from the pressure, but she was unaware of the pain she inflicted. Her leg muscles tightened, her feet sliding the few inches along the bench until her toes pressed against his thigh. ''How could it not be your child?''

''Easy. I never slept with her.'' His gaze was fierce, intent on hers. ''Never, Nikki. I never slept with her.''

''Never?''

"Never. Not before we were married, and not after we married." He covered her feet with one big, warm hand, then reached out with the other to tuck a strand of hair behind her ear.

The gesture was so gentle, his fingers slowly brushing her ear as he withdrew his hand, that it shook Nikki's barely held composure more than if he'd grabbed her and kissed her.

"That's one of the reasons you're so angry at me, isn't it? You thought I was seeing Marguerite, having sex with Marguerite, while we were dating?"

"Yes." Nikki couldn't deny it. The knowledge had broken her heart, left her bitter at the betrayal.

"Well, it's not true."

"I don't understand any of this," Nikki said shakily. "Why would you have married her if you weren't the father?"

"I can't tell you. The story doesn't belong to me alone. It involves other people, and it could ruin their lives."

"Do I know these people?"

"I can't answer that."

Nikki struggled to understand, but she couldn't come up with any scenario that would force Cully to marry a woman he didn't love, a woman carrying a baby that wasn't his.

"And you expect me to believe this on what...? Faith alone?" Her voice was incredulous.

"I know it's a lot to ask."

"And you also expect me to believe that the night we spent together meant something to you, but you walked away from any future we might have because of something terrible involving other people? But you can never tell me what it was nor who the people are?''

''I know it sounds crazy.''

''Crazy? It sounds like the plot for a really bad movie.''

He ran his fingers through his hair and clasped the back of his neck, an endearing half grin curving his lips. ''You're right, it does. Unfortunately...'' he sobered, his gaze intent ''...it's also true.''

She drew a shaky breath. ''So—where does that leave us?''

His somber gaze darkened. ''I hope it leaves us with you a little less angry. I can't change the past, Nikki. And even if I could, given the same set of circumstances, I'd marry Marguerite. I know it's too much to expect you to forgive me or to forget what happened, but I'm hoping that you'll stop hating me quite so much. Maybe enough to make it possible for you to tolerate being in the same room with me so Angelica won't worry.''

''I don't know. I...'' She stared at him, unable to form a coherent response, still grappling with what he'd told her.

''If it helps at all, the marriage was hell. The only good that came of it was that I learned I make a lousy husband and an even worse father. I'll never make that mistake again.''

''It doesn't help,'' she murmured.

''No,'' he agreed. ''I guess it doesn't.''

The silence stretched. The muted sounds of music and laughter from down the block were gone. No traffic sounds disturbed the quiet of the wide residential street.

"Well, that's it then," he said at last when she remained silent. He bent, retrieved his hat and stood in one fluid motion. "I didn't come here tonight to tell you this so you'd forgive me, Nikki. I know that's not going to happen. I hoped that if I told you as much as I'm free to tell, it might make it easier for you to accept my being around. For Angelica's sake," he added, his voice gruff.

"Thank you, Cully."

"You're welcome."

Unspoken words, unvoiced yearnings and regrets, filled the air between them, sexual tension heightening the atmosphere until Nikki could barely breathe.

"Good night." He turned on his heel and stalked away, boot heels echoing on the porch boards.

"Good night," Nikki murmured after him.

He didn't slow down, merely lifted a hand in acknowledgment as he strode down the steps. Moments later, the pickup's taillights flickered as he braked for the turn at the end of the block. Then he was gone, the engine noise fading away on the still night air. Quiet fell over the neighborhood, wrapping around Nikki on the shadowed porch.

Her thoughts were far from quiet.

Could it be true? She remembered the look on his face as he'd told her that their night together had been important to him, and later when he'd told her he had no choice but to marry Marguerite.

Nikki was convinced he hadn't lied. But if he was telling the truth, she couldn't imagine a set of circumstances that could have compelled him to marry a woman pregnant with another man's child.

Why would he do it?

She was still sitting on the porch, deep in thought, when Cora arrived home just after midnight and urged her up the stairs to bed.

Nikki didn't sleep well, shadowy dreams waking her throughout the predawn hours. She woke the next morning to find sunlight slanting through the window and across the floor, telling her that the hour was far past her normal rising time.

She tossed back the covers, fumbled down the hall to the bathroom to brush her teeth, wash her face and drag a brush through her hair before making her way downstairs for coffee.

The kitchen was empty, but the aroma of freshly brewed coffee filled the big room. Nikki opened one of the old-fashioned cupboard doors and went up on tiptoe to reach a mug. It wasn't until she poured, sipped, sighed and leaned against the counter behind her that she realized she wasn't alone.

Cully stood in the screened-in back porch just off the kitchen, a carpenter's tool belt slung around his waist and a hammer in one hand. He wasn't wearing a shirt, she realized dazedly, following a trickle of perspiration as it slipped over the washboard muscles of his abdomen to disappear beneath the waistband of his faded jeans, which was dragged lower by the weight of the tool belt.

When she dragged her fascinated stare back up his body to his face, she realized that he was watching her with eyes so hot she was surprised the mesh in the screen door separating them hadn't melted.

And she realized that anger no longer protected her from the heat between them. She'd hated Cully Bowdrie for the last four years with the same level of intensity that she'd once loved him. Bitterness had been her constant companion. Now it was gone, as completely as if it had never been, banished by his cryptic explanation and leaving her vulnerable to him once again.

"Good morning."

His deep, faintly raspy voice startled her from her thoughts and she flushed, realizing that she had no idea how long she'd been staring at him.

"Good morning." Her own voice was husky. "What are you doing here?" *He knows,* she thought, nearly panicking as she read the speculation in his narrowed eyes. Cully was too primal not to sense the shift in her response to him.

He nodded toward the outside screen door. "Cora mentioned that the door was sticking and I promised her I'd take a look at it."

"Oh."

Cully wondered if she realized how tempting she was. He'd heard her enter the kitchen, and had stopped working to watch her. She was wearing a pink crop-top and shorts in some kind of clingy stuff—he guessed they were pajamas—and when she stretched to reach a mug, the top slid up to bare her tanned abdomen and the bottom swell of her breasts.

"Would you like some coffee?" she asked.

He knew he should stay on the porch side of the screen door, but the need to get closer had him unbuckling the tool belt and dropping it and the hammer on the floor before he stepped into the kitchen.

"Sure."

She turned to set her mug on the counter, and once again Cully was treated to the sight of her stretching on tiptoe to snag a mug. He moved up behind her, his body caging hers against the counter. She went completely still, the curve of her bottom nudged by his jean-clad thighs, her shoulders pressed by his bare chest.

"Here, I'll get that." He easily reached the shelf and grabbed a mug, setting it down before he braced his hands on the countertop on either side of her. Her hair tickled his chin and he bent his head the few inches necessary to reach her. "You smell so good," he muttered, breathing in the clean, flowery scent of shampoo.

"Cully, you shouldn't—"

"Shh. I know." He nuzzled her nape and felt her shudder. His hands left the counter and reached for her, one splaying over her belly to press her closer against him, the other finding the soft, bare skin under the short knit top.

Her breath hitched.

"Where are Aunt Cora and—" she caught her

breath again when his hand moved, brushing higher beneath her top "—and Angelica?"

"They walked downtown. Cora said she needed milk," he murmured, his mouth tasting the soft skin of her throat.

"They'll be back soon," she managed to say.

"Then we don't have a lot of time," he muttered.

He turned her around, his mouth covering hers, his arms wrapped around her to fuse her against him, from breast to thigh.

It wasn't a tentative kiss. It was a kiss fueled by weeks of wanting and not having, of dreaming and being denied. Her mouth opened under his and his tongue thrust deep, claiming and taking possession.

Nikki didn't know when she wrapped her arms around his neck and speared her fingers through his hair. Her senses were on overload, the sensitive tips of her breasts pressed against his chest with only a layer of thin cotton separating them, her short pajama top riding up to leave the bare skin of her abdomen fused against Cully's.

A lawnmower started up outside, the engine noise intruding into the kitchen.

Nikki tore her mouth from his and pressed her hot face against his shoulder. "We have to stop," she groaned, shudders shaking her.

"In a minute," he muttered, his mouth stroking across her cheek.

"No. Now." She planted her hands against his shoulders and pushed. He allowed her to put a few inches between their upper bodies, but their hips and thighs were still pressed together.

"What?" he asked, his eyes heavy-lidded, his face flushed with color.

"I'm not ready for this, Cully."

He shifted restlessly, the hard length of his arousal pressing higher against the notch of her thighs. She shuddered and nearly whimpered with the need to drag him down onto the floor.

"I mean it." Her fingers clenched over the curve of his shoulders. "I'm not ready."

His gaze met hers, his body taut with denial. Then he released her and slowly, carefully, eased his weight from her until they were no longer touching.

"Are you going to be? Ready for this?" The words were taut, strained with the effort it had taken to move away from her.

"I don't know," she whispered. "I believe what you told me last night, Cully. But I don't know if I can do this again. You hurt me so badly last time that I wasn't sure I was ever going to be okay again."

He winced, his entire body flinching at her words. "I'm sorry, Nikki. So damn sorry." The words were torn from him, the pain her statement caused him etched on his face.

"I need time," she repeated, not knowing what else to say to him.

"All right." He nodded, tight-lipped.

Angelica's chattering sounded outside on the front lawn.

"They're home."

Cully crossed the kitchen, pausing with the

screen door held open to look back at her. "I don't want you to feel uncomfortable around me while you're thinking about this. But Angelica wants to dig in my garden later this morning. Will you come out to the ranch with her?"

"Yes."

"Good."

With one last hot stare, he turned and left the house.

Nikki stared after him for one mesmerized moment before the sound of Cora and Angelica chatting over the side fence with Junior brought her to life.

She grabbed her coffee cup and hurried back upstairs to the shower.

Chapter Nine

Nikki and Angelica spent countless hours at Cully's ranch over the next two weeks. Part of the time they spent clearing flower beds and cleaning the garden; part of the time was taken up with riding lessons for Angelica. Cully didn't press Nikki, but he took every opportunity to touch her, brushing against her as he passed and standing so close that their bodies touched when they talked. She was always aware that he watched her, and she watched him, absorbing the gentle care he used when teaching Angelica and the firmness he applied when the girl was fractious.

Nikki spent the nights alone, repeatedly going over the little information he'd given her until her head ached. She wouldn't ask Cully to break his silence and tell her all the reasons he'd felt compelled to marry Marguerite, so that left it up to her to work them out.

Until one night, long after everyone else was asleep, long after she'd turned out the lights, she realized with a flash of insight that there was only one person in the world who could have made Cully marry against his will.

Quinn. It had to have been Quinn.

The Bowdrie brothers were fiercely loyal. Cully would take a bullet for Quinn if necessary, she thought, trying to remember what Quinn had been doing that summer.

Courting Victoria. He was courting Victoria.

A swift image of Cully smiling with pleasure four years ago as he told her that his big brother had finally fallen head-over-heels in love flashed before her eyes.

And Quinn had been dating Marguerite before Victoria came to town. Could Marguerite have been pregnant with Quinn's child?

Nikki sat up in bed, hugging her knees, as she examined her theory from every possible angle.

It made sense, she decided finally. She frowned. But why couldn't Cully tell her? The car crash that had taken Marguerite's and the baby's lives had happened nearly three years ago. How could any of that hurt Quinn now?

A plausible reason to explain Cully's insistence that other people could still be hurt didn't come to her, no matter how many ways she tried to approach the problem.

The only possible solution was to confront Cully with her theory, but she was unwilling to do so until she decided what to do about the sexual web that daily drew tighter around them.

So Nikki let the days slide by, enjoying Cully's and Angelica's company and drawing no closer to a decision.

One Saturday night nearly a week after her late-night revelation, Nikki was the sole person awake in the big old house. Cora and Angelica had long since gone to bed. Too restless to watch television, read or sleep, Nikki walked into the kitchen, switched on the light and took a handful of cookies from the jar next to the toaster. She pulled open the refrigerator's magnet-dotted, white enamel door and checked the top shelf, only to discover that the sole container of milk was nearly empty.

"Rats," she muttered aloud in the quiet kitchen. "No milk. I can't eat double chocolate chip cookies without milk."

She returned the cookies to the ceramic jar, flipped off the overhead light and left the kitchen. Slipping her bare feet into the sandals she'd left just inside the front door earlier, she took a five-dollar bill from her wallet, tucked it into the pocket of her khaki shorts and left the house.

A quick glance at her watch told her that it was only a few minutes after ten o'clock. She took her time walking the few blocks to the nearest mini-mart. The night was shadowy, the moon that rode high in the sky a slim quarter sickle. The spreading branches of tall maple trees on lawns threw darker pools of shadow across the sidewalk. Nikki walked in and out of the splashes of cool moonlight and warm shadow until she reached the gas station–grocery store with its bright lights. The parking lot was empty except for one red sedan as Nikki crossed the pavement and pushed open the door to the small shop. The red leather strap studded with bells that hung on the inner door handle jangled as Nikki stepped inside.

"Hey, Nikki."

"Hi, MaryLou." She waggled her fingers at the owner's wife and headed down the aisle toward the refrigerated case set against the back wall.

MaryLou Burton, with a voluminous white grocer's apron wrapped around her thick waist, went back to stocking shelves.

Nikki located the milk section and pulled open the heavy door, a wave of frigid air greeting her.

"Cully Bowdrie's fighting again."

Nikki's head lifted, her attention snared by the comment, her fingers curled around the handle of a plastic milk carton. Several feet to her left, MaryLou tucked a box of candy bars onto the shelf and relayed the latest bit of gossip to Monica Sanderson.

"Again?" Monica shook her head at the announcement and added a bag of pretzels to the six-pack of soda cradled in her arms. "That man starts brawling every year about this time. It's getting so a person can almost set her calendar by him. Who's he fighting with this time?"

"Jackson Rand. He's the man who inherited the Kuhlman place when old Eli passed on last year."

Monica pursed her lips with appreciation and gave a soft wolf whistle. "Oh, yeah. I've seen him. The guy's a hunk. Of course," she added, "so is Cully Bowdrie. Someone ought to tell those two that they'd be better off not marking up those handsome faces. Besides, aren't those two neighbors?"

"I believe so—I think Kenny told me that their ranches share a fence line."

"What are they fighting about?"

"Darned if I know. Kenny didn't say. He was in such a hurry to get over there and watch that he hung up the phone before I could ask him for all the details."

"Men." Monica rolled her eyes. "I've never understood why they love to watch other men fight."

"Me, either. It must be one of those things only males understand. Kenny said half the men in town are standing on the sidewalk next to the hardware store, and he had to stop talking to me because he was missing all the fun."

Nikki didn't stay to hear more. She shoved the plastic gallon container of milk back into the minimart's refrigerator case and hurried out of the store.

What in heaven's name was Cully doing? If what Mrs. Burton said was true, Cully went through this every year.

Nikki walked quickly, lengthening her stride until she was nearly running down Main Street. Several blocks away, the streetlight in front of the closed, dark hardware store threw a pool of light

over a crowd of men on the sidewalk that edged
the empty lot next door. She was only half a block
away when the small crowd shifted and moved,
breaking up.

Oh, no. Onlookers never left until a fight was
over. Anxiety spurred her into a run until she was
forced to slow in order to dodge men near the
empty lot.

She caught a brief glimpse of a tall man with
sandy hair, blood smeared across his cheek beneath
a swollen eye, as he stepped into the street. Nikki
could see that dust coated his shirt and jeans, but
then he moved away, crossing the dark street.

Although the man certainly looked like he'd been
fighting, he wasn't Cully. She quickly dismissed
him, her gaze searching the crowd until she found
a familiar broad back and black hair beneath a straw
cowboy hat on the far side of the crowd, moving
away from her. She sidestepped the shirt-and-tie-
clad Mr. Fredericks, Colson's portly banker, and
hurried after Cully. He was walking fast, his strides
longer than hers, and she ran to catch up, halting
him with a hand on his arm.

He spun around, hands lifting and curling into
fists before he recognized her. His arms dropped
back to his sides and he glared at her. "What the
hell are you doing here?"

"I heard you were fighting."

"Yeah? Well, you heard right. Go home."

"Not unless you come with me." She caught his
chin in her hand and turned his face more fully to
the light, wincing as she did so. Although the night

shadows painted his face in shades of gray, there was enough light that she could see the damage Jackson Rand's fists had done. Blood oozed from a cut over Cully's cheekbone and smeared across his jaw. His lower lip was swollen, and Nikki suspected that it, too, had been cut, while his right eye looked bruised.

"Oh, Cully, what have you done?"

He stared at her without blinking. Beneath her hand, his body vibrated with leashed tension. "What does it look like?"

"It looks like you need to see a doctor." She spoke softly, conscious of the violence that still rode him.

"I don't need to see a doctor. There's nothing wrong with me."

"Cully, you've got a cut that looks like it needs stitches," Nikki protested.

He jerked away from her hand. "I don't need stitches."

"All right. Come home with me and I'll check your cuts. If we can get the bleeding stopped, you won't have to go to the emergency room for stitches."

"I'm not going home with you."

"Look, if you don't trust me, then we'll have Aunt Cora take care of you. She's great with cuts and bruises."

"I'm not dragging your aunt out of bed to wipe blood off my face," he snarled. "And I'm not going near your house where Angelica might see me."

"Oh." That he would think of her little sister at this moment and consider her reaction to his fighting caught at Nikki's heart. She thought swiftly. "Very well," she said with quick decision. "Then I'll go home with you."

"No, you won't."

"Yes, I will. I'm not letting you out of my sight until I'm sure that you're okay."

"There isn't anything wrong with me that a little cold water and a couple of days' healing won't fix."

"Maybe." Nikki met his fierce glare without flinching. "But I'm not budging. You either come home with me or I'm going home with you."

He swore, one brief, succinct word.

Nikki ignored him. She folded her arms across her chest and stared at him.

"All right, dammit," he muttered. "But you'll ride with me and I'll drive you home after you've finished playing nurse."

"Fine." Nikki didn't bother telling him that she would drive herself home, using his pickup, after she was sure that he didn't need stitches.

"My truck's this way." He cupped her elbow in his palm and strode down the sidewalk.

Nikki nearly ran to keep up with him. Fortunately, he towed her along with him for barely a block before he stopped next to a truck and yanked open the passenger door. She climbed in and he closed the door with controlled force. Moments later, he slid beneath the steering wheel.

He turned the key and the dash lights came on,

the soft glow faintly illuminating the cab's interior. Nikki paused in the act of fastening her seat belt to inspect his face, and caught her breath in an audible gasp.

Cully flicked her a quick, sidelong glance. "Stop worrying." He shifted the truck into gear, the tires biting pavement with a quiet squeal as he accelerated.

Nikki bit back a worried protest, focusing instead out the window as the powerful truck quickly left behind the nearly deserted streets of Colson.

Cully didn't speak. The silence inside the truck was deafening. Nikki glanced at him. His right hand rested on the floor gear shift, the skin on the back of his knuckles torn and rusty with dried blood.

He reached out and turned on the radio. The mellow voice of George Strait filled the cab, eliminating any possibility of conversation.

The miles flew by in silence. It wasn't until Cully parked in front of his house and helped Nikki out of the truck that he spoke. "The first aid kit is in the bathroom off the kitchen."

He held the gate for her, waiting until she passed through before he followed her up the walk to the front porch.

Nikki had seen the solid two-story house often in the daytime, but the structure took on an unfamiliar strangeness at night, its roof and corners darker lines against the gloom. Beneath the overhanging porch, the shadows cast by the quarter-moon deepened. Cully waved her ahead of him into the house, but the darkness was so thick that she couldn't see a thing.

"Wait."

Cully's hand closed over her shoulder and she halted abruptly, her senses heightened by the total blackness.

"I'll turn on a light. Stay here."

His hand lifted, and with it, the warmth radiating from his body to hers disappeared. Nikki mourned the loss.

She heard a click and a lamp flared to life, the soft glow illuminating the room.

"The kitchen is this way," Cully said.

She knew the layout of the first floor from her visits with Angelica and their trips to the kitchen for water, but she didn't comment. Instead, she followed silently as Cully led her down a short hall to the back of the house. He switched on an overhead light as they entered the kitchen.

"The bathroom's through the utility room."

He gestured across the kitchen. The bright light revealed that his face and hands were far more battered than Nikki had originally thought.

"You look awful." Her eyes narrowed as she searched his face. "And your lip is bleeding."

"Thanks for telling me." He scrubbed his hand over his mouth, wincing when the movement pulled at his split lip, and looked at his fingers. A streak of crimson stained the tips.

"Sit down," Nikki ordered.

He glared at her, clearly considering refusing, before he gave in. Snagging a chair from the table, he pulled it out and dropped onto the seat, lifting a brow at her.

Satisfied, Nikki turned on her heel and walked quickly through the utility room to the small bathroom. The medicine cabinet over the sink yielded a bottle of prescription pain pills and a first aid kit with antiseptic and bandages, while the cabinet below held washcloths and hand towels. She returned to the kitchen to find Cully slouched in the chair, his eyes half-closed.

"Cully? Are you all right?"

He opened his eyes and scowled at her. "Of course I'm all right. I'll be even better when you finish fussing over me so I can get some sleep. I've been up since 5:00 a.m. chasing Rand's cattle out of my pasture."

Reassured that he wasn't going to pass out, Nikki deposited bottle, bandages, towel and washcloth on the table and walked to the sink. "Is that what you were fighting about? His cattle in your pasture?"

"Yes."

Nikki rummaged in a lower cupboard and found a large bowl. "And that was worth the two of you getting black eyes and bruised knuckles?"

"Hell, yes," Cully snarled. "This isn't the first time his cattle have gotten into my pasture. If he'd replace his fences I wouldn't have to waste days shagging his cattle out of my pasture and back into his. Where they belong."

"Hmm." Nikki filled the bowl with warm water and set it on the table next to him. She dropped the terry washcloth into the gently steaming bowl and wrung out the excess water. "Tip your head up."

Cully scowled at her but did as she bade. His gaze fastened on her face as she cupped his chin in her hand and gently smoothed the warm damp cloth over the cuts and bruises on his face.

"Ouch." He flinched away from her hold when she dabbed at the cut on his cheek.

"Hold still." She frowned, carefully washing away the dust and dried blood. "I think you need stitches in this, Cully."

"Just stick a Band-Aid on it."

She glanced up, her gaze snared by his, startled that he was so near. "It's probably going to leave a scar."

His mouth twisted in a half grin that didn't reach his eyes. "It won't be the only one."

"Hmm." Nikki turned away, ostensibly to rinse the cloth in the bowl of water, while in reality she needed time to calm the shiver of nerves racing down her spine. She wrung out the cloth and returned to the task of wiping dust and blood from his face. She smoothed the cloth over his temple and he closed his eyes, the right one swollen and bruised. "You're definitely going to have a black eye."

He grunted a noncommittal response.

Nikki yanked open the freezer door on the double-door refrigerator and scanned the contents, locating a plastic bag of frozen peas.

She bumped the door closed with her hip, her hands busy twisting the plastic to break apart the frozen chunks of peas inside until the bag was flexible.

"Here." She covered his eye with the bag and caught his right hand in hers, lifting it to the bag. "Hold that."

He sucked in a breath in a surprised hiss. His one good eye narrowed at her and he lifted the cold bag so he could look at it.

"Peas? You're putting peas on my eye?"

Nikki firmly guided his hand and the bag back to his eye. "The peas are frozen. They make a perfectly good ice pack."

"Hmm." He returned the cold bag to his eye.

Nikki was relieved when his good eye closed and she was released from his disturbing gaze. It gave her the freedom to study his features without him being aware that she did so. The weariness that darkened the skin beneath his eyes and etched lines at the corners of his mouth hadn't been caused by the fight with his neighbor.

"You've been working too hard," she murmured, concentrating on scrubbing the last of the dust and blood from his skin.

"No more than usual," Cully responded. The cold pack was beginning to ease the burn in his eye, and the warm cloth stroking his face, combined with the gentle touch of Nikki's fingers as she turned his face slightly, lulled him with the sheer comfort of having someone care for him. Normally, he drove home alone, stuck his head under cold running tap water, slapped a Band-Aid on any cuts that refused to stop bleeding, and fell into bed, aching and lonely.

"This might sting a little."

Cully barely heard her words, but the firm touch of a cotton swab soaked with antiseptic woke him with a vengeance. His good eye snapped open and he glared at her.

"What the hell are you doing?" he roared.

"Don't be such a baby. I just put a little hydrogen peroxide on the cut on your cheek."

"Next time, warn me first."

She raised a brow at him. "I did. You weren't listening?"

He muttered something under his breath and closed his eyes again. Nikki carefully applied a butterfly bandage to the cut over his cheekbone, frowning at the depth of the wound.

"I still think you should get stitches for this," she commented, carefully smoothing the ball of her thumb over the adhesive.

"I don't."

"Fine. Be stubborn."

She pulled a chair out from the table and plunked it down facing Cully. She rinsed out the washcloth and sat down, shaking out the hand towel and placing it over her thigh. Then she reached across him and picked up his hand.

Cully nearly groaned aloud when she stroked the warm cloth over his palm and between his fingers. But when she lay his hand, palm down, on her thigh to more easily wash his split knuckles, it was all he could do not to push the towel away and ease his hand over her silky skin and beneath the hem of her khaki shorts.

Her hands on him were driving him crazy. He was torn between wanting her to keep touching him and pushing her away before he did something they'd both regret.

Nikki was having her own problems dealing with touching Cully. The urge to lean forward and kiss all the sore, bruised places on his beloved face warred with the inclination to berate him for brawling in the first place. She forced herself to focus on cleaning his bruised, torn knuckles, her head bent over her task to avoid his brooding gaze.

"There." Satisfied that she'd done all she could, Nikki moved his hand from her thigh to his knee and stood, shaking out the damp towel. "That's all I can do if you refuse to get stitches."

Cully's only response was to glare at her in silence.

"Well, then..." She crossed to the sink, pulled open a cabinet door, found a glass and filled it with tap water. She shook out one of the pain tablets from the bottle she'd found in Cully's medicine cabinet and handed both glass and tablet to Cully.

"What's this?" he asked suspiciously.

"Basically, really strong aspirin."

He tossed the tablets into his mouth and drank, his throat moving rhythmically as he swallowed, draining the glass. He rose to return the empty glass to the sink, then headed for the door.

"Where are you going?"

He paused, glancing over his shoulder. "To the truck. I'm taking you home."

"You can't."

His eyes narrowed and he turned slowly until he faced her. "I can't? Why not?"

"Because the instructions on the pill bottle said you shouldn't drive after taking them."

"I thought you told me they were extra-strength aspirin?"

"I said they were basically aspirin—there are a few other ingredients. One of which makes you drowsy, so you can't drive after taking it."

He stared at her without blinking, a muscle flexing in his jaw, the silence ominous.

"I can drive myself home, Cully. I told you I would." She held out her hand for the keys.

Cully's hand closed into a fist, the truck keys locked inside, and with slow, controlled movements, he shoved them into his jeans pocket.

"It's nearly midnight on a Saturday night and you are *not* driving home alone."

"I'm a grown woman, Cully. I'm perfectly capable of driving myself home."

"No," he said flatly. "The only way you're leaving this ranch is if I drive you."

Nikki eyed the rigid set of his chin, the glitter in his green eyes, and was suddenly conscious of the quiet of the house, the isolation of the ranch.

"Now, Cully—" she began.

"Don't try to talk me out of this," he interrupted. "Either I drive you home or you stay here. Which is it?"

"You know I can't let you drive after I gave you those tablets," she all but yelled in frustration.

"Fine." He shoved the door closed and stalked toward her, catching her hand in his to tow her after him.

"Hey!" She tried to pull away from him, but had no success in loosening his grip as she half ran to keep up with his long strides. "What are you doing? Where are we going?"

"Upstairs to bed."

Her heart stopped beating for one shocked moment before she caught her breath and it shuddered into a heavy, throbbing beat once again.

"Bed?" The word came out in a choked gasp.

"Yes, bed. It's after midnight. I've been up since before dawn chasing those damn cows of Rand's. I'm tired."

He strode down the upstairs hall, giving Nikki no chance to voice the question she needed to ask. Then he threw open the door to a bedroom and shoved her inside. She had time for one wild glance around the neat room before he turned his back and left. She could hear his boot steps as he crossed the hall, heard the noise of drawers scraping open.

She was standing exactly as he'd left her when he reappeared in the doorway.

"Here." He tossed a T-shirt at her. "You can sleep in this."

He pulled the door shut, leaving Nikki staring at the wooden panels, speechless. His boots thudded across the hall, then the door slammed. She heard a few muffled thumps and then silence reigned.

Her heart settled back into a slower rhythm. A distinct sense of anticlimax swept Nikki and, much as she didn't want to acknowledge it, keen disappointment.

Part of her wished, deeply wished, that Cully had hauled her upstairs to share the bed across the hall.

Sighing, she turned away from the door, her gaze sweeping the room. To her surprise, it was neat as a pin, the bed covered with a simple green spread, the pillows propped against the dark oak headboard. The oak nightstand matched the bed as well as the tall dresser standing against the wall.

She crossed the room and dropped the white cotton T-shirt on the bed. A book lay on the nightstand next to the green ginger jar lamp with its cream shade. Curious, Nikki picked up the leather-bound volume, opened it and found Victoria's name written in flowing black script inside the cover.

"Ah, I should have guessed," she murmured, her gaze moving slowly once again over the neat room, assessing the cream drapes that matched the pleated shade on the lamp and the gleam of new oak furniture. She'd bet her last dollar that Victoria had chosen the furnishings for this room. Nikki couldn't envision Cully choosing the almost feminine furnishings, let alone coordinating the greens of the bedspread and lamp and the cream tone of the drapes and lampshade.

Victoria had clearly claimed this room in Cully's home for herself and Quinn. Nikki felt a quick spurt of warmth at the evidence that Cully had family that cared for him, and she wondered if Victoria and Quinn's daughter had the bedroom next door.

Nikki pulled the scoop-necked cotton T-shirt off over her head and draped it on the back of the small armchair next to the window before she walked back to the bed and unhooked her bra, letting it slip down her arms to fall on the bed. She dropped Cully's white T-shirt over her head and slipped her arms through the sleeves. The extra-large shirt hit her at midthigh and the shoulder seams fell halfway to her elbows, the neck opening slipping to one side to bare a shoulder.

She tugged it back into place and glanced in the mirror, smiling at the picture she made in the too-big shirt, before she unzipped her shorts and stepped out of them.

Bra and shorts joined her shirt on the small armchair before she crossed to the hall door and eased it open to peer out. The door across the hall to Cully's room was closed tight, no glimmer of light visible where door panels met doorjamb.

Relieved, Nikki tiptoed down the hallway and crept down the stairs. Although she hated to waken her aunt, she knew that if she didn't call and tell Cora where she was, the older woman would worry.

Certain that she remembered seeing a phone on the kitchen wall earlier, Nikki felt her way down the dark hallway from the stairs to the kitchen. Moonlight found its way into the room through the uncurtained window over the sink. Although the light was dim, it was enough for Nikki to locate the telephone on the wall just inside the door. The light was even dimmer there, however, and she struggled to read the numerals as she punched in Cora's phone number.

The phone rang several times before Cora picked up.

"Hello?" Her voice was raspy with sleep.

"Aunt Cora—"

"Nikki?" Cora's voice sharpened. "Is that you?"

"Yes."

"Why are you whispering? Come to think of it, why are you calling me on the phone? Where are you?"

"I'm at Cully's ranch."

"Cully's ranch?" Cora's voice reflected bewilderment. "I thought you were downstairs watching a movie."

"I was. But I went out to get milk and—"

"In the middle of the night?"

"I know it sounds a little strange, but I wanted milk to drink with chocolate chip cookies, and the container in the fridge was nearly empty. So I walked down to the minimart to buy a gallon, which is where I was when I overheard MaryLou telling Monica Sanderson that Cully was fighting."

"Fighting?"

"Yes," Nikki sighed, knowing full well that her explanation was probably only confusing Cora more. "It's a long story, Aunt Cora, but he split his lip and cheek and he has a black eye. I wanted him to come back to the house with me, but he didn't want Angelica to see him like that, so he refused. So I made him bring me home with him.''

''I see.''

Nikki could tell by her aunt's confused tone that Cora didn't see at all. ''I'm sorry to wake you so late, Aunt Cora, but I didn't want you to worry if you discovered that I wasn't at home. I'll stay the night here and Cully will drive me home in the morning.''

The telephone line fairly vibrated with her aunt's unasked questions, but Nikki didn't want to explain further. Even though she was whispering, she was worried that Cully might waken and come downstairs to investigate. She didn't want to face him again in the darkened kitchen, certainly not dressed as she was in nothing but a T-shirt and undies.

''I'll tell you all about it tomorrow, Aunt Cora. I have to hang up now. I don't want to wake Cully.''

''All right,'' Cora agreed, a little of the sleep gone from her voice. ''But we're definitely going to discuss this, Nikki.''

''Yes, Aunt Cora.'' A quick grin curved Nikki's mouth. Her aunt's tone told her that her explanation had better be good. Nikki suspected that she would never grow old enough to be beyond her aunt's mothering. ''Good night.''

''Good night.''

Nikki replaced the receiver with a barely audible click and moved quietly out of the kitchen, tiptoeing up the stairs and down the hall to her open bedroom door. She slipped inside and eased the door closed behind her with careful movements.

It wasn't until she was in bed with the sheet and blanket tucked beneath her chin that she drew a deep breath of relief, knowing she'd reached the safety of her bed undetected. Her eyelids grew heavy, snapping open again when a tree branch rubbed against the wall outside the window. The creakings of the old house startled her several more times before sleep pulled her under.

Cully woke before dawn. He turned his head on the pillow and looked out the window, wincing when the movement pulled the bruised and cut skin of his face. Night was easing into predawn gray outside, the faint light making it possible to see the shapes of furniture in his room.

He shifted onto his side, groaning as sore muscles protested, and bunched the pillow beneath his head. His fingers grazed cold metal and he frowned in confusion.

What the hell? He wrapped his hand around the metal shapes and drew them out from beneath the pillow, staring at the metal ring and four keys.

Memory flooded back and he groaned out loud, closing his eyes as he remembered hauling Nikki upstairs and dragging her into the empty bedroom across the hall.

Great, Bowdrie. Smart move.

He wondered if she was still asleep there or if she'd found a way to leave. He couldn't remember a thing after shedding his boots, jeans and shirt and falling into bed.

He'd drank exactly one beer at the Crossroads. Nowhere near enough to make him fall asleep so swiftly or so deeply, and he wondered just exactly what was in those pills that Nikki had told him were only "strong aspirin."

And he wondered just how angry she was going to be at him this morning for refusing to give her his truck keys last night.

Not that he'd been wrong about that. He scowled at the gradually lightening ceiling.

Damned if he thought it was safe for her to drive the miles between the ranch and town after midnight by herself. The road was deserted at that hour. It wasn't safe. Anything could happen. What if the truck blew a tire, or a deer ran into the road and caused her to crash?

No. He'd been right not to let her drive back to town alone, but he'd also been a jerk, he thought bleakly.

Damn.

He threw back the covers and rose, aching in more places than he could believe.

Rand must have landed more punches than I remember. A quick glance out the window revealed his truck, still parked in front of the house. Which meant that Nikki must still be asleep across the hall.

He opened bureau drawers and collected underwear, socks and jeans before grabbing a shirt off a hanger in the closet. Then he eased open the hall door. The door opposite him was closed, the hallway quiet.

Cully made his way down the stairs to the bathroom shower off the utility room, determined not to waken Nikki. Truth was, he didn't want to face her any sooner than necessary, because he knew very well that he was going to have to apologize. He wasn't looking forward to it.

The shower's hot water eased some of the aches from his battered body, and hot coffee chased from his brain the last of the fuzziness induced by Nikki's tablets.

He carried his second mug of coffee through the living room and onto the front porch, leaving the inner door open and carefully easing the screen door closed behind him. Bands of pink edged the horizon, declaring to the world that dawn was on its way.

This was Cully's favorite time of day, when the dark night, with its dreams that were too often filled with the scream of twisting metal and the coppery taste of blood, were banished by the sunlight. He didn't dream during the day, but then, he never slept during the day. And as the end of summer and the anniversary of the time his life had fallen apart drew near, followed by the date of the car wreck, he slept less and less.

The squeak of the screen door opening behind him interrupted his moody contemplation of the horizon. His muscles were already tightening with anticipation before she spoke.

"Cully?"

He half turned to look over his shoulder.

Chapter Ten

Nikki stood in the open door, silhouetted against the dim light from the hallway. Her hair was ruffled, her eyes slumberous. Her right hand held the screen door open while her left held together the edges of a cream-colored blanket. The cream wool wrapped around her shoulders and draped to the floor, gaping open to reveal the long length of her bare legs from midthigh to toes.

She looked sleepy, vulnerable and too damned appealing. He thought he'd grown used to the quick slam of desire that hit him every time he saw her, but the deep sense of satisfaction and contentment that poured through him now was new. Having her with him at the beginning of the day felt so very right.

Cully fought the urge to pick her up and carry her back upstairs to her warm bed.

"Kind of early for you to be up, isn't it?" His voice was still gravelly from sleep. "Did I wake you?"

"No, I don't think so. I'm not sure why I woke, but once I did I couldn't go back to sleep." She stepped forward, letting the screen door slap softly shut behind her. "How are you feeling this morning?" She crossed the porch and halted a few inches away, scanning his face.

Cully winced. "If you're talking about the cuts and bruises, I feel fine."

The blanket slipped, sliding off her right shoulder, and Nikki absentmindedly tightened her hold. The predawn darkness was growing lighter by the minute, allowing her to see Cully's face more clearly. His eye wasn't quite as swollen this morning, but the bruises on his face were darker, the cuts red and angry against his suntanned skin.

"You don't look fine." Concerned, she frowned at him.

He leaned against the porch's support post, one hand tucked into his jeans pocket and the other holding a gently steaming mug.

"Trust me, this is nothing." He shrugged. "I've had worse."

Nikki's gaze moved over the raw-looking skin of his knuckles before returning to trace the bruises and cuts on his face. "You've changed so much," she murmured. "I don't remember ever hearing about you fighting four years ago, Cully. What happened?''

Nikki felt his withdrawal as surely as if he'd flinched away from her, even though he didn't actually move a muscle.

''I told you. I had a few words with Jackson Rand about his lack of fences. He objected and we both threw a few punches. That's all.''

''Gossip says you get in fights every year about this time.''

''And you believe it?''

''Not if you tell me it isn't true.''

He was silent for a long moment. ''I can't tell you it's not true,'' he said at last.

She waited, her gaze fastened on his.

''Oh, hell,'' he said at last. ''You aren't going to give up until you get an answer, are you?''

She shook her head.

''The answer is simple. I hate this time of year. Makes me cranky. And I usually wind up in a few fights. It's never anything serious.'' He glared at her. ''Trust the gossipy old biddies in Colson to make a big deal over it. You'd think they'd find something better to talk about.''

She blinked slowly, confusion written across her face. ''This time of year makes you cranky? You mean the weather? The heat bothers you?''

Cully groaned and scrubbed his hand down his face. ''I should have known you wouldn't accept a simple explanation,'' he growled. ''I hate this time of year because exactly two weeks from today is the anniversary of the day you left Colson.''

"Oh." A faint frown creased her brow. "You get cranky every year around the date I left?" The frown slowly gave way to a growing smile. "Is this a backhanded way of telling me that you were upset when I left?"

Without taking her gaze from his, Nikki stepped forward until her bare toes nudged his own, rested the palm of her hand against his chest for balance and rose on tiptoe to kiss the underside of his chin.

His eyes narrowed, his heart thudding faster beneath her palm. "Don't do that unless you mean it."

"I mean it," she whispered.

"Does this mean you're done thinking about us?"

"Yes."

"And what have you decided?"

"That I've wasted a lot of time thinking."

He smiled slowly, his eyes going dark. "It's about damn time." He set his coffee mug on the porch railing and bent to slip an arm under her legs, swinging her off her feet and into his arms.

She gasped and clutched at him, gaining a fistful of shirt. "Where are you taking me?"

"Where you belong," he said, his voice raspy, deeper. "To bed."

He yanked open the door and started up the stairs, her blanket trailing behind them. Moments later, he kicked open the door to his room, crossed to the bed and set her on her feet. Without speaking, he ripped open his shirt and shrugged out of it, letting it fall forgotten to the floor as he grabbed the hem of the big T-shirt and pulled it up over her head. He grew still, his eyes hot as he took in her tousled hair, flushed face and the bare curves covered only by a scrap of white bikini panties.

"I've dreamed of you like this for years," he muttered as he reached out and wrapped his arms around her, slowly drawing her closer until her nearly nude body rested against his. Her arms circled his neck, the soft weight of her breasts pressing against his chest, and he groaned. His palms smoothed down her back and he lifted her, bending his knees slightly to align the soft notch of her thighs with his. His mouth took hers.

Nikki went under without a thought of saving herself from the flood of passion that slammed into her. They were nearly naked, but it wasn't enough, not nearly enough. She squirmed, trying to get closer, and his big body tensed, his arms tightening just before he picked her up and dropped her gently on the bed.

Startled, she pushed herself up on her elbows. "Hey. Where are you going?"

"Nowhere, honey. Let me get my clothes off." His voice was thick, reassuring.

He shed his jeans with swift movements and crawled over her, settling her beneath him, his hair-roughened thighs sliding over hers.

His head lowered and he nuzzled her throat just below her ear, his lips tasting the soft skin before he found her earlobe and licked it gently. "You should have been here weeks ago."

"I know," she gasped softly, her eyes closing at

the wet heat of his mouth on her earlobe. "We could have…ohhh."

He released her ear, his lips moving unerringly across her cheek.

Nikki's lashes lifted, her breath catching. The damage to Cully's battered face was even more startling up close.

"Oh, Cully. Your poor face." Cradling his head between her palms, she brushed soft kisses over his swollen eye. "Does it hurt terribly?"

"Not when you do that." He lifted his hand, brushing his rough knuckles against her lips. "Want to make these better, too?"

"Don't fight anymore, Cully," she murmured, smoothing her lips over the torn skin.

"If you'll keep doing that, honey, I'll promise you anything," he muttered, the heat in his eyes flaring as she gently sucked his fingertip. "I cut my lip, too."

"Poor baby." Nicki smiled, tugging his head down.

He took her mouth with fierce heat and Nikki gasped, her body arching against his as his tongue found hers. Cully wrapped an arm around her waist, his other hand cradling her head, and crushed her closer as his tongue thrust deeper into her mouth. She wound her arms around his neck, her fingers moving with greedy pleasure over satiny skin. Muscles flexed and shuddered beneath her touch. His hair was soft, the strands cool against her fingertips, in sharp contrast to his nape, which was hot beneath her palms.

His lips left hers and brushed down the arch of her throat to test the rapid pounding of her pulse at the base of her neck. Nikki felt the butterfly brush of his lashes against her skin as he moved lower, trailing openmouthed kisses over the swell of her breast. Then his mouth closed over the tip, and the hot, wet suction as he drew on her sent her body curling reflexively into his, her hands cradling his head, pressing him closer.

He groaned, his arms tightening almost painfully before he shifted to the side and his hand left her waist, stroking down her hip and thigh. He hooked his thumb in the elastic of her panties and stripped them down and off over her toes.

The heated sexuality that held Nikki in its fevered grip burned higher, as Cully rose over her, nudging her knees apart to make a place for himself between them. His much bigger male body crowded hers against the mattress, blanketing her, and his lips covered hers, his tongue surging into her mouth at the same time his body invaded hers.

Nikki gasped, struggling to accept him, her muscles clenching against the invasion.

"Easy, honey." His voice was thick, his body shuddering with the effort it took to go still. "Relax, baby, let me in."

His hand brushed across her belly and into the nest of curls between her thighs, searching for and finding the sensitive knot of nerves. Nikki jerked at the flood of heat, surging against him, and he slid fully inside her. Both of them caught their breath at the nearly unbearable pleasure, then Cully began to move.

Much later, Nikki curled against his side, her head on his shoulder and palm on his chest.

"It was Quinn, wasn't it?"

He tensed, his fingers tightening on her thigh where it lay across his. "What was Quinn?"

"The reason you married Marguerite."

"What makes you think it was Quinn?"

She sighed, tilting her head back to look up at him. "Cully, the only person in the world that you love enough to give up your life for is Quinn."

"Not the only person," he muttered, his lashes lowering until only a flash of dark green fire could be seen.

Nikki's heart caught. "No?"

"No." The silence thickened between. "You're right," he said at last. "I married Marguerite because of Quinn."

"Tell me."

"I swore I'd never tell anyone. If I tell you, you can never tell Victoria or Quinn."

"I promise," she said solemnly.

He dropped a swift hard kiss on her mouth, then dropped back with Nikki still entwined in his arms.

"Quinn used to see Marguerite off and on before Victoria came to Colson. To be blunt, neither of them were married, and they had a mutually agreeable association for occasional sex. He'd been seeing her off and on for the better part of a year. Then he met Victoria and he fell in love. I've never seen

Quinn like that with a woman. He was crazy about her.''

"I remember." Nikki smiled wistfully.

"Then you know how he was about her. Quinn's a lot like our father." Cully shifted, pulling her closer. "Charlie never got over losing our mother. He searched for her until he died, and he was miserable every day of his life after she left. I knew that if Quinn didn't marry Victoria, his life would be ruined."

"So you married Marguerite instead of Quinn?"

"Yeah. She came to the ranch looking for Quinn the morning after you and I made love. Quinn wasn't home, thank God."

"But you were?"

"Yes. I made her tell me why she insisted on seeing Quinn, and she said that she was three months pregnant with his kid. She didn't give a damn that he was involved with someone else. She said he had to marry her."

"But surely she couldn't have forced him to marry her?"

"You don't know my brother, honey," Cully said grimly. "He has a conscience the size of the state of Montana, and he's stubborn as a mule when it comes to kids growing up without a parent. He would have married her, all right. And he would have lost Victoria and been a miserable son of a bitch for the rest of his life. I watched my father go through that—married to Eileen and sick with misery over losing my mother. I couldn't let that happen to Quinn."

"So you married her instead."

"Yeah. She didn't care which of us she married, just as long as her husband was a Bowdrie. It was public knowledge that Charlie left a will giving any of his descendants a right to part of his estate, and Marguerite planned to get rich."

"But she didn't live long enough to enjoy the money."

"No. And she wouldn't have had access to the estate anyway," he said grimly. "Because the baby wasn't Quinn's."

Nikki's eyes widened. "Oh, no. So you wouldn't have had to marry her?"

"Not in the final analysis. But I couldn't have known that earlier, so I would still have married her."

"When did you find out that the baby wasn't Quinn's?"

"In the hospital after the car wreck. I wanted to donate blood, but we didn't match." He threaded the silky strands of her hair between his fingers. Comforted by the soft weight of her body lying against his, for the first time he found himself able to think about the nightmare of the car wreck that haunted his dreams. "I made her sign a prenuptial agreement so that she had no individual claim against the estate through the marriage, and she agreed to have blood tests done to prove paternity as soon as the baby was born. But she kept delaying, coming up with a thousand excuses why she couldn't have the tests done. I kept insisting. That's what we were fighting about the day of the wreck."

"What happened?" Nikki held her breath, wondering if he would tell her.

Cully was silent for long moments. "I was fed up with her putting me off with one lame excuse after another. I told her I was driving to Missoula on business and she could ride along with me if she wanted to go shopping. After we got in the car, I told her I'd made an appointment at the hospital to have blood drawn for the tests. She started screaming and hitting at me, and then she grabbed the wheel. I tried to stop her, but she yanked the wheel and kicked my foot on the accelerator. The car left the road and we started rolling. I don't know how many times we rolled before the car slammed into the ravine. She was screaming, bleeding from cuts from the windshield glass. The baby didn't make a sound."

Cully paused, the horrific scene playing out in front of him once again.

"I was wearing my seat belt, but Marguerite took hers off earlier, just before she started hitting me." Cully didn't want to remember the fury and bitter resentment he'd seen in her eyes.

He stopped speaking, his breathing choppy, and Nikki pressed closer, her arms tightening around him.

"She bled to death, begging me to save her, and cursing me with the next breath."

"But you survived."

"Yes. A car full of tourists stopped and one of them knew some first aid. They stopped the bleed-

ing and raced me and the baby to the hospital. But
they couldn't save Marguerite.''

"Thank God they arrived in time to save your
life,'' Nikki breathed.

"I'm the only one that survived,'' he said grimly.
"The boy was in bad shape and I wanted to donate
blood for him at the hospital. That's when I learned
that he couldn't have been Quinn's kid because
Quinn's blood and mine are the same type. His
didn't match.''

"Cully, I'm so sorry.''

"So am I. Sorry I couldn't save him. Sorry I
couldn't save her.''

Nikki tipped her head back and searched his face.
His features were set in harsh lines, his eyes bleak.
"But you did all you could. Surely you can see
that?''

"It wasn't enough.''

"I know. But you're not Superman. You were
injured. In fact, you nearly died from your injuries,
didn't you?'' She smoothed her palm over the scar
that marked his throat and chest. "How could you
possibly have done any more than you did?''

Nikki knew from the unrelenting set of his face
that her words weren't convincing him. He was
eaten up with guilt, and her heart ached for him.

"Cully, you have to believe me,'' she said, trying
once more to convince him. "You're punishing
yourself for something that no one could have prevented. It's obvious you feel responsible for the
death of Marguerite and her baby, but you know
you'd never expect the same of anyone else had

they been in your position." Tears welled and overflowed, to trickle unheeded down her cheeks. Nothing she said made the slightest bit of difference in how Cully felt about his culpability. He was stubborn, overly conscientious and impossibly dear.

"Hey." His face softened and he stroked the dampness from her cheek before bending to kiss her mouth. "Don't cry. Not for me." He pulled back and looked at her.

Bare inches separated their faces, hers vulnerable and worried, his somber and intent.

"I learned something about myself in the last four years, Nikki. I'm no different than my father and brother. Bowdrie men only love once. I lost you once and it was hell. I'll be damned if I'll let you get away this time. I know I'm a bad bet for a husband, Nikki, and you'd be crazy to forgive what happened before, but I can't let you go. Please, marry me."

"Marry you? You want to marry me?" Nikki was stunned.

"Hell yes, I want to marry you." He frowned at her. "What did you think this was about?"

"I don't know," she managed to answer, happiness bubbling through her veins. "Another one-night stand?"

"We've never had a one-night stand," he growled.

"No," she agreed. "We haven't. But it was a very, very long time between nights."

"Too long." Closing his fingers on her thigh, he pulled her knee higher so he could nudge his hips against hers, his arousal stroking her soft, heated center.

Nikki gasped and buried her hot face against his throat, distracted.

"Way too long," he muttered, the need to bury himself inside her roaring with demand until he could barely think. He forced himself to go still. "Say yes." He tipped her face up and kissed her. "Say you'll marry me, Nikki."

"Yes." Her fingers closed around him and he shuddered.

"Thank God." He ground out the words as he pulled her beneath him.

Nearly a year later, Colson once again simmered under the hot summer sun.

Cully was impatient to make his bride-to-be his wife, so Nikki enlisted Cora and Victoria to help with preparations. The whirlwind of activity resulted in a wedding that had Colson gossips smiling for months. Even Cully, reluctant as he was to wait even a week to wed Nikki, had to admit that the sight of his beautiful bride, dressed in white silk and lace, walking down the church's red-carpeted aisle to the altar, was something he'd never forget. And when Angelica proclaimed that Petersen women were not only good gardeners, but also beautiful brides and flower girls, he agreed wholeheartedly.

Cully sat in an old-fashioned oak rocker on his front porch, Nikki curled in his lap. Across the neatly trimmed lawn in the shade of the big old maple, Cora and Angelica knelt at the edge of a flower bed, with pots of brilliant annuals waiting beside them to be transferred to newly turned soil.

He dropped a kiss on Nikki's temple and smiled when she curled closer. "I want to adopt Angelica, Nikki."

Startled, Nikki tilted her head back to meet his solemn gaze. "You do?"

"Yes. I want her last name to be Bowdrie. Do you mind?"

"No." She slipped her arms around him and hugged him tight. "Not at all. I think it's a wonderful idea."

"How do you think Angelica will feel about it?"

"I think she'll be delighted. She adores you, Cully, and several times since she learned that you share Charlie as a father, she's asked me why you and Quinn have a different last name than hers."

"What did you tell her?"

"That our mother chose the name for her birth certificate, and she picked Petersen instead of Bowdrie. Angelica seemed to accept that reasoning, so I didn't explain further. But I think she'll be very happy to switch to Bowdrie. Except…" She glanced across the lawn at the two industrious gardeners and smiled. "She won't be able to quote Cora's favorite saying about Petersen women being gardeners."

"Maybe she could keep Petersen and add Bowdrie—Angelica Rose Petersen Bowdrie. It's a lot of names for a little girl, but do you think she'd like that better?"

"That's an idea," Nikki replied. "And Aunt Cora might like to have her keep the Petersen name."

"Good." Cully absentmindedly threaded silky strands of her hair through his fingers while he stared at the two Petersens, one young, one old, busily moving dirt and planting flowers. "You Petersen women have done wonders with this old place."

"We have, haven't we." Nikki's voice held satisfaction. The house gleamed with new paint, both inside and out, and the rooms were filled with comfortable furniture and a profusion of green and flowering plants. "I love my kitchen."

"Yeah." A smile curved his mouth. "I had an ulterior motive for remodeling that kitchen."

"I know you did. The more I putter in the kitchen, the happier you are. Sometimes I think you only married me because I can cook." She tilted her head back to look up at him, brown eyes alight with laughter.

"Hmm." He pretended to consider her accusation. "You know," he admitted in a slow drawl, "that might have been one of the reasons, but it wasn't the most important one."

He bent his head and pressed his open mouth against the upper curve of her breast, bare above the white cotton tank top she wore. His palm left her knee and slipped beneath her gathered skirt, stroking up her inner thigh.

"Cully!" Nikki gasped and grabbed his hand,

glancing across the lawn. Cora and Angelica were focused on the flower bed.

''What? They can't see us.'' He kissed her ear and settled his hand over her barely rounded abdomen. ''When are we going to tell them about the baby?''

''I'd like to keep it just our secret for a little while longer. Do you mind?''

''No, honey. I don't mind.'' His hand moved in small, soothing circles. ''Are you sure you're okay with this? Being pregnant when your business is so new?''

''Absolutely,'' Nikki reassured him. ''I love the consultant work I'm doing at senior citizens' residential complexes, but I'm perfectly content to put it on hold while I'm carrying our baby. So stop worrying, okay?''

''Whatever makes you happy.''

Her dark eyes took on a calculating gleam. ''Anything?''

''Anything within reason.'' He eyed her expression and groaned. ''Oh, no. What now? Don't tell me you want pickles dipped in peanut butter again. Just thinking about that combination turns me green.''

''I was thinking more along the lines of strawberry shortcake smothered in whipped cream.''

''Now that's more like it.'' He slipped his arms under her legs and back and stood. ''And after we eat the shortcake, I've got other ideas for the leftover whipped cream.''

''Cully!'' Nikki pretended to be scandalized, but laughter completely ruined the effect.

The screen door eased shut behind them, and in the shadowy hall, Cully kissed her. Sheltered in his arms, his child growing beneath her heart, Nikki knew that she'd come home at last.

* * * * *

These *New York Times* bestselling authors
have created stories to capture the hearts and minds
of women everywhere.
Here are three classic tales about the power of love—
and the wonder of discovering the place
where you belong....

FINDING HOME

DUNCAN'S BRIDE
by
LINDA HOWARD

CHAIN LIGHTNING
by
ELIZABETH LOWELL

POPCORN AND KISSES
by
KASEY MICHAELS

*Available only from Silhouette
at your favorite retail outlet.*

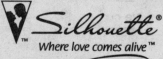

Silhouette®
Where love comes alive™

This Mother's Day Give Your Mom A Royal Treat

Win a fabulous one-week vacation in Puerto Rico for you and your mother at the luxurious Inter-Continental San Juan Resort & Casino. The prize includes round trip airfare for two, breakfast daily and a mother and daughter day of beauty at the beachfront hotel's spa.

INTER·CONTINENTAL
San Juan
RESORT & CASINO

Here's all you have to do:

Tell us in 100 words or less how your mother helped with the romance in your life. It may be a story about your engagement, wedding or those boyfriends when you were a teenager or any other romantic advice from your mother. The entry will be judged based on its originality, emotionally compelling nature and sincerity. See official rules on following page.

Send your entry to:
Mother's Day Contest

In Canada	**In U.S.A.**
P.O. Box 637	P.O. Box 9076
Fort Erie, Ontario	3010 Walden Ave.
L2A 5X3	Buffalo, NY
	14269-9076

Or enter online at www.eHarlequin.com

PRROY

HARLEQUIN MOTHER'S DAY CONTEST 2216
OFFICIAL RULES
NO PURCHASE NECESSARY TO ENTER

Two ways to enter:

• **Via The Internet:** Log on to the Harlequin romance website (www.eHarlequin.com) anytime beginning 12:01 a.m. E.S.T., January 1, 2002 through 11:59 p.m. E.S.T., April 1, 2002 and follow the directions displayed on-line to enter your name, address (including zip code), e-mail address and in 100 words or fewer, describe how your mother helped with the romance in your life.

• **Via Mail:** Handprint (or type) on an 8 1/2" x 11" plain piece of paper, your name, address (including zip code) and e-mail address (if you have one), and in 100 words or fewer, describe how your mother helped with the romance in your life. Mail your entry via first-class mail to: Harlequin Mother's Day Contest 2216, (in the U.S.) P.O. Box 9076, Buffalo, NY 14269-9076; (in Canada) P.O. Box 637, Fort Erie, Ontario, Canada L2A 5X3.

For eligibility, entries must be submitted either through a completed Internet transmission or postmarked no later than 11:59 p.m. E.S.T., April 1, 2002 (mail-in entries must be received by April 9, 2002). Limit one entry per person, household address and e-mail address. On-line and/or mailed entries received from persons residing in geographic areas in which entry is not permissible will be disqualified.

Entries will be judged by a panel of judges, consisting of members of the Harlequin editorial, marketing and public relations staff using the following criteria:
- Originality - 50%
- Emotional Appeal - 25%
- Sincerity - 25%

In the event of a tie, duplicate prizes will be awarded. Decisions of the judges are final.

Prize: A 6-night/7-day stay for two at the Inter-Continental San Juan Resort & Casino, including round-trip coach air transportation from gateway airport nearest winner's home (approximate retail value: $4,000). Prize includes breakfast daily and a mother and daughter day of beauty at the beachfront hotel's spa. Prize consists of only those items listed as part of the prize. Prize is valued in U.S. currency.

All entries become the property of Torstar Corp. and will not be returned. No responsibility is assumed for lost, late, illegible, incomplete, inaccurate, non-delivered or misdirected mail or misdirected e-mail, for technical, hardware or software failures of any kind, lost or unavailable network connections, or failed, incomplete, garbled or delayed computer transmission or any human error which may occur in the receipt or processing of the entries in this Contest.

Contest open only to residents of the U.S. (except Colorado) and Canada, who are 18 years of age or older and is void wherever prohibited by law; all applicable laws and regulations apply. Any litigation within the Province of Quebec respecting the conduct or organization of a publicity contest may be submitted to the Régie des alcools, des courses et des jeux for a ruling. Any litigation respecting the awarding of a prize may be submitted to the Régie des alcools, des courses et des jeux only for the purpose of helping the parties reach a settlement. Employees and immediate family members of Torstar Corp. and D.L. Blair, Inc., their affiliates, subsidiaries and all other agencies, entities and persons connected with the use, marketing or conduct of this Contest are not eligible to enter. Taxes on prize are the sole responsibility of winner. Acceptance of any prize offered constitutes permission to use winner's name, photograph or other likeness for the purposes of advertising, trade and promotion on behalf of Torstar Corp., its affiliates and subsidiaries without further compensation to the winner, unless prohibited by law.

Winner will be determined no later than April 15, 2002 and be notified by mail. Winner will be required to sign and return an Affidavit of Eligibility form within 15 days after winner notification. Non-compliance within that time period may result in disqualification and an alternate winner may be selected. Winner of trip must execute a Release of Liability prior to ticketing and must possess required travel documents (e.g. Passport, photo ID) where applicable. Travel must be completed within 12 months of selection and is subject to traveling companion completing and returning a Release of Liability prior to travel; and hotel and flight accommodations availability. Certain restrictions and blackout dates may apply. No substitution of prize permitted by winner. Torstar Corp. and D.L. Blair, Inc., their parents, affiliates, and subsidiaries are not responsible for errors in printing or electronic presentation of Contest, or entries. In the event of printing or other errors which may result in unintended prize values or duplication of prizes, all affected entries shall be null and void. If for any reason the Internet portion of the Contest is not capable of running as planned, including infection by computer virus, bugs, tampering, unauthorized intervention, fraud, technical failures, or any other causes beyond the control of Torstar Corp. which corrupt or affect the administration, secrecy, fairness, integrity or proper conduct of the Contest, Torstar Corp. reserves the right, at its sole discretion, to disqualify any individual who tampers with the entry process and to cancel, terminate, modify or suspend the Contest or the Internet portion thereof. In the event the Internet portion must be terminated a notice will be posted on the website and all entries received prior to termination will be judged in accordance with these rules. In the event of a dispute regarding an on-line entry, the entry will be deemed submitted by the authorized holder of the e-mail account submitted at the time of entry. Authorized account holder is defined as the natural person who is assigned to an e-mail address by an Internet access provider, on-line service provider or other organization that is responsible for arranging e-mail address for the domain associated with the submitted e-mail address. Torstar Corp. and/or D.L. Blair Inc. assumes no responsibility for any computer injury or damage related to or resulting from accessing and/or downloading any sweepstakes material. Rules are subject to any requirements/limitations imposed by the FCC. **Purchase or acceptance of a product offer does not improve your chances of winning.**

For winner's name (available after May 1, 2002), send a self-addressed, stamped envelope to: Harlequin Mother's Day Contest Winners 2216, P.O. Box 4200 Blair, NE 68009-4200 or you may access the www.eHarlequin.com Web site through June 3, 2002.

Contest sponsored by Torstar Corp., P.O. Box 9042, Buffalo, NY 14269-9042.